The Guide of Time

Book I: The Journey

By: Cinzia De Santis

The Guide of Time.

Book I: The Journey

ISBN-13: 978-9956282-2-9

For Sayo, a true Guide of Time

Most of the characters and events

in this novel are fictitious.

Some of them are not,

and readers will know which is which.

Contents

Prologue: How it all began..1

Chapter 1...12

Chapter 2...18

Chapter 3...29

Chapter 4...42

Chapter 5...51

Chapter 6...54

Chapter 7...62

Chapter 8...70

Chapter 9...76

Chapter 10...84

Chapter 11...91

Chapter 12...99

Chapter 13...105

Chapter 14...111

Chapter 15...117

Chapter 16...125

Chapter 17..131

Chapter 18..139

Chapter 19..145

Chapter 20..158

Chapter 21..168

Chapter 22..181

Chapter 23..184

Chapter 24..195

Chapter 25..200

Chapter 26..203

Chapter 27..207

Chapter 28..211

Acknowledgments.....................................214

About the book 215

About the Author..218

Bibliography:..219

Other Sources 221

Connect with me:.......................................222

Prologue: How it all began

21st century

The elderly editor, beard now largely grey, was staring at the document in his hands. For the first time in his publishing career, he was lost for words. In the chair opposite him, an old woman was smiling at him, almost as though she was enjoying his discomfort. He raised his eyes and frowned at her. Her name was Ariane Claret. The thought crossed his mind that she must have been a beautiful woman when she was young.

—Is all this true? I mean, did it really happen?

—Yes, it's true —she said calmly.

—How can you prove it? How can I make sure what you have given me is real? We don't publish fiction, you know. We publish science books, proper science.

—Some of the book is about historical events. You can check the facts on them yourself.

—Yes, I'm not worried about the verifiable events, but what about the rest?

The woman shrugged her shoulders.

—The rest is true as well. Publishing the book would announce what is starting to happen. It's the right time.

—Are you one ... one of them?

The woman chuckled, and the editor couldn't help but think that whatever the truth, she was a most intriguing woman.

—No, I am not one of them —her face was suddenly serious—. But I know them well.

—Aren't you afraid this story might make you look ridiculous?

—At my age, I have nothing to lose, and besides, the events to come will prove me right. But let me tell you how it all started. Even if I can't convince you, let me at least try to entice you.

***

Siberia, Ice Age

It was winter, an unusually cold winter, and it wasn't until late in the afternoon that Huuks and his tribe finally reached the cave. The older people had slowed down their progress, and two women had given birth during the journey. Huuks knew they were still being followed, but at least he had now found some temporary safety. They were running away from the Nuwooks, a fierce tribe that was rapidly expanding across the steppes where Huuks used to live. The Nuwooks were faster and stronger and they had more powerful weapons; worst of all, they were cannibals. They massacred all the males in the tribes they conquered, and took the women. Huuks knew his tribe was in mortal danger.

Although it was the coldest time of the year and they had little food for the journey, in the middle of the night they had left their settlement and headed for the mountains where they could hide.

Huuks had recently become the leader of his tribe when his father was killed by a mammoth. He was ready to take over: he was the most skilful hunter and the best fighter. But Huuks was more than that, much more. He could find his way through forests and across open plains just by listening to the sounds of the Earth; he knew how to soothe physical pain by using his hands; he could smell a plant and tell whether it was poisonous or edible. Often he woke up in the middle of the night with visions of things that went on to happen. He could anticipate when his tribe was at risk from enemies or when a place wasn't going to provide enough food. Thanks to Huuks, his tribe had survived while several others had perished.

Huuks was also deeply curious. He studied his surroundings, and while his followers took most things in nature for granted, he wanted to know more. He was mesmerised by the bright points above his head in the otherwise blackness of the night, the water falling on his face when the sky thundered, the swish of the air when it crossed the forest, the beauty of a flower, the harmony of a bird's song. Sometimes the world scared him, but mostly he was in awe.

He had discovered the cave by chance some time ago after leaving his tribe temporarily to follow a strange deer with only one horn. It was a beautiful animal with thick white fur. Huuks had never seen anything like it before, and the white deer seemed to want to be followed.

Huuks chased it across the steppes and into a forest, where he headed for some thick vegetation and pushed it aside to reveal the entrance to a cave. Cautiously, Huuks peered inside, but it was too dark to see anything. Just as he was about to turn away, he saw two bright eyes staring at him from the darkness.

Huuks was startled; those didn't look like deer eyes. A moment later, they disappeared, and he was left puzzled and even more curious. But Huuks had to get back to his tribe. As he turned to leave, he failed to notice a big rock at his feet; he tripped, fell to the ground and lost consciousness.

When Huuks woke up, he was outside the cave, his head aching. He had to return to his tribe, but he would remember the way to the cave. When the time came to run away from the Nuwooks, he chose to lead his tribe to it.

Now they were there, hungry and cold, but at least they were safe. It was pitch black when they arrived. They shared some raw meat and roots and soon the women, the old men and the children were asleep. Huuks and the other young men in the tribe stayed near to the entrance of the cave, ready to protect them. Huuks himself slept outside the cave. Not even the Nuwooks could take away from him the joy of looking at the bright spots of the night.

***

Many miles underground, in a bright room with monitors covering the walls, and dominated by a control centre, Huuks and his tribe were being watched. A dozen people dressed in bright metallic clothes were staring at the screens, noting every movement in and around the cave. Their features were similar to those of the people they were watching, though their eyes were brighter and their frames slimmer; after all, they had a common ancestor. But mentally and emotionally, they couldn't have been more different. The Seers' society had evolved through knowledge and collaboration, based on harmony and mutual support, unlike other species of humans. They were a peaceful nation, free of crime, where greed and desire to dominate were unknown. The Seers could foresee events that would harm them and that was a reason why their lives were much, much longer.

—They have arrived —said Ammuri, in a calm voice. He was operating the monitors and shifting the focus of the cameras to different parts of the cave, paying particular attention to Huuks.

—It's time —said Hospere, an elder woman with deep blue eyes and obviously in charge—. Are you ready, Ammuri?

—Yes, I am.

—Are we sure this is the right decision? —intervened Ristiori, his challenging tone filling the room. His opinion mattered, not least because he directed all the surface expeditions and had himself been "up to the outside" on several occasions, but this time it would be different.

Ammuri would face new risks he might not be ready to deal with.

—We made the decision a long time ago, Ristiori — replied Hospere, her voice quiet but firm.

Ristiori looked at her, wanting to insist on his point, but he sensed her determination and the mood of the others in the room, and bowed his head in agreement. He knew that the decision had been taken and he felt deep respect for Hospere. Still, he was worried about the consequences of getting in touch with such a primitive species. The Seers didn't use any form of violence against themselves or others, and they abhorred the killing of living creatures. It was against their laws and it was against their nature. But humans on the surface usually reacted violently to other species, which they considered a potential threat.

—They need us —continued Hospere.

—It's hard to believe they are still so backward — murmured a young woman sitting by Ammuri's side, hypnotised by what she saw on the screen in front of her.

—We were able to develop a more advanced society — said Hospere—. Other species of humans couldn't. It is time for us to intervene in their evolution and help them choose the right path. We need to make sure the planet is safe both for them on the surface and for us underground.

A hum of excitement spread across the room. After thousands of years, this would be the first time that one of them was leaving the world they had created underground to make contact with the humans on the surface, and the prospect was both thrilling and scary.

After a moment of shared exhilaration, Ammuri returned to his pragmatic concerns. For the umpteenth time, he ran through his mental checklist of the expedition he was about to embark on. Although he had gone through rigorous training to prepare for this mission, he had spent nearly all his life in a world of shadows.

The sunlight at the surface could have devastating effects not only on his eyes and skin but also his vital organs. But the top danger would be oxygen concentration, which he knew could easily damage his lungs. He would have to give himself plenty of time to adapt, and he would have to rely on special equipment. He knew that the next few months – years? – wouldn't be easy, but he was thrilled that he would be the first of his kind to make contact with humans.

Ammuri —said Ristiori, interrupting his thoughts—, we will be following you closely. Make sure you are always in contact with us, even when you are asleep. If at any point you feel you aren't safe, you will come back. Likewise, if I ever feel you are not safe, I will order you to return.

—I understand, and I will do as you say —replied Ammuri, as he turned around and looked again on the monitor at the place where he had to venture.

—It's time for us to share the news with the Council of Elders and the rest of our community —said Hospere as she walked out of the room with others. She looked at Ammuri and smiled. She knew what he was thinking and she was pleased.

A light vehicle was waiting outside the room to take Hospere to the Council of Elders, the seat of the Seers' Government, a few hundred miles away. After a quick journey through the well-lit tunnels, she entered a six-storey building where the Elders —the ruling body of the Seers, chosen from the wisest among them— were waiting for her. They greeted her enthusiastically; they had been waiting for the news for a long time.

—This is a crucial moment in our history and in the history of humans —Hospere began—. One day, when we are able to reveal ourselves, this will be remembered as the beginning of a new era for the Earth. We have identified the individual we want to contact. He is the leader of a small tribe that lives in the steppes, and Ammuri will soon to go to him.

A murmur ran through the room. Hospere continued:

—As you know, we agreed this was the right decision. It's in our nature to share knowledge and to seek improvements in our lives until we are called to the Higher Light. Also, we are inhabitants of the same planet as the people on the surface. We have always made sure that what we do does not threaten life on the surface, and in the same way, we don't want their life to threaten ours. Our mission is to guide other species of humans to their bright destiny and steer them away from the darker path. They need our influence, our help.

The Elders rapidly blinked their eyes to show their excitement.

—This news fills our hearts, Hospere —said one member of the audience—. What will be the first step we will take? What will Ammuri teach them?

Hospere's reply was brief.

—How to produce fire.

***

After several days in the cave, Huuks felt that for the time being they were safe from attack. But they were starving, and above all terribly cold. Some children and elderly people had already died. At night, he and a handful of other men stole out of the cave to go hunting, but they hadn't killed enough to feed everybody or to get enough furs to warm them up. One night, after another unsuccessful hunt, Huuks was lying outside the cave staring at the bright spots in the sky when he saw a light approaching in the forest. He grabbed some stones and threw them towards the light, but nothing happened and it kept getting closer. The glow was yellow and intense. When it was just a few metres away from the entrance to the cave, the light stopped. Huuks was scared, but intrigued. He had seen something similar before, but never that close. He walked cautiously towards the light. As he got closer, he realised it was coming from a small bunch of sticks and leaves. He reached out to touch it, and felt a searing pain in his hand. His first impulse was to run away, but despite his throbbing fingers, his curiosity got the better of him. He walked towards the light again, and this time he came closer without touching it. It felt nice; his body was feeling more comfortable. As long as he didn't get too close, the light made him happy.

All of a sudden, he was overcome by tiredness and lay down on the ground. He was used to sleeping only lightly, always alert in case of a predator or an enemy. But this time he had one of his vivid dreams: he saw a strange figure looking at him, holding two sticks of wood that he started rubbing together. In Huuks's dream the sticks started to produce the same light he had seen in the forest. The strange figure put the light on a small bunch of dry leaves and it flared up, so big that it seemed to reach the sky. The figure put his hand towards the fire and he smiled.

Huuks woke up immediately, and there was the light, still in front of him. In the darkness, he looked for pieces of wood like the ones he had seen in the dream. Then he started rubbing one against another. For what seemed like an age, nothing. Just when Huuks was thinking of giving up, there suddenly was the light! His triumphant howl reverberated through the forest. Many miles underground, watching the monitors in their meeting room, Hospere and the Elders were excited too. The first step to guiding mankind had been successful. The dynasty of the Guides of Time was born.

***

When she finished telling the story, Ariane looked at the editor and asked with a smile:

—So, have I convinced you? Have you decided what to do?

The old man gazed at her. He noticed the brightness of her eyes, glowing like green stars even in the afternoon twilight.

—I am going to read the manuscript again, and then I will give you an answer.

—Fine —she said, standing up—. I'll wait for your call.

With as much eagerness as he'd ever felt before, the editor turned over the first sheet of the document and began to read.

Chapter 1

Bormia (Malta), 20th century

The first memory I have of my childhood is the smell of detergent. In the orphanage where I grew up, the nuns who ran it were as strict about hygiene as they were about their religious duties. Cleanliness was the eleventh commandment. Perhaps they thought it would banish all the smut and sin from the minds of the young girls who lived there.

The orphanage was a two-storey building in a wood on a hill, next to the convent where the nuns lived. The closest village, Bormia, with its white houses and cobbled streets was half an hour away, near a sandy beach where, on special occasions, the nuns would take us to spend the afternoon.

The nuns told me I was born in September, but they didn't know the exact date. My mother had given me away soon after I was born and then disappeared. The nuns called me Ariane and registered my last name as Claret, the name of the saint protector of the order they belonged to. There were usually about 20 girls in the orphanage, and all of us longed to find a family who would adopt us. Sunday was the day that might happen —the parade, we called it— and our hopes rose as the end of each week drew near. I must have been about three when I first went on the parade —or at least this was the first time I can remember. A nun came to collect me from the dormitory and, in silence, I walked along the long corridor to the visiting room, holding her hand tightly.

It wasn't long before those visits became a real torment. Nobody wanted to adopt me. Once I heard a nun saying it was because I was too different. I looked in the mirror: with my reddish curls, pale skin and dull-green eyes, why would anyone want me? In a country full of light and colour, of people with brown skin and coal-dark eyes, I was just too odd.

Once I thought I had got lucky. I spent a few days with prospective parents. But then they took me back to the orphanage, and shortly afterwards chose another girl. For nights on end, I cried myself to sleep. Then, as I was getting over that sadness, Alma came running into the dormitory and threw her arms around me:

—I am leaving, I'm leaving! —She cried with excitement.

Alma had grown up with me in the orphanage. She was my only friend.

—When? —I asked, my heart sinking. I had seen too many times other girls in the same mood, their happiness matching my own gloom.

—Soon, I'm going to another country, with snow and lots of toys —Alma said, jumping up and down. Then she stopped and looked serious for a moment:

—Can you come with me?

—I don't think so —I replied, holding back tears.

—I'll come back for you —Alma said, a big smile on her face—. You will come and live with me.

The day Alma left, I stayed up late looking out the dormitory window, waiting for her. I waited for months, but she never came back.

It was during that period, though, that I made a new friend. I had just fallen asleep, troubled and unhappy, when I was suddenly aware of somebody standing by my bed. I saw a slight figure, with plaits in her hair and a finger to her lips smiling at me.

—Sshh —she whispered—. You must be Ariane. My name is Eliza.

I wondered if I was dreaming. She was a complete stranger, but seemed to understand my surprise.

—Don't be scared —she said—, I know you have never seen me before, but I sleep during the day and the nuns don't know I'm here.

—Are you also waiting to be adopted? —I asked.

—No, I am here just to be your friend —she replied—. Look, I have a lizard in my pocket.

Eliza produced it, bright green in the moonlight, and put it on the floor. She gave it some food and said:

—His name is Lucky.

—Can I touch it? —I asked, fascinated.

—I have one for you —she said, putting her hand in her pocket again—, yours is blue.

The second lizard looked at me, almost as though it wanted to say something.

—What's his name? —I whispered. —Theodore —she said—, but you can call him Theo. Then she walked quickly away from my bed. I thought I must have been dreaming, but Theo was definitely there. I put him carefully in a box, and the next morning I brought him a grasshopper I had caught outside. I spent the rest of the day longing for the night, when Eliza might visit me again. I could hardly wait to see what would happen. And sure enough, Eliza suddenly appeared by my bed, just as she had done the previous night. This time I was wide awake. She had a frog for me, she said, and over the next week it was followed by mice, worms and even a little bird. And in a way that I couldn't understand, they all seemed to do whatever she asked: the frog jumped high, the mice ran round in circles, the worms coiled up.

Eliza told me the story of her fascinating life. During the day, she went to the village and stayed with a very old lady —hundreds of years old, she said— who taught her how to speak to animals. Also, the old lady taught Eliza how to read minds. In fact, one of our favourite games was for Eliza to guess what I was thinking.

—A chocolate cake! —she said, the first time we played. She was right. I had once eaten some delicious chocolate cake on a brief outing with a family that might have adopted me, and I couldn't stop thinking about it.

15

I decided to mention Eliza to Sister Ines, the only nun I trusted, but she looked at me as if I were crazy. After that, I didn't tell her about the little zoo under my bed and for some strange reason, the nuns never found out.

One Christmas, women from the village came to give us used toys. I wasn't impressed by the dolls or the miniature saucepan, but then I saw a little piano on the floor. The other girls fiddled with it for a while, before turning their attention to the dolls.

I touched one of the keys, and then another, and the sound that came out of it seemed like magic. I started spending every minute I could with the tiny piano, and it didn't take me long to start playing the basic notes of the hymns we sang in church. Sister Ines —before becoming a nun, she had dreamt of being an opera singer— was in charge of the convent's choir and encouraged me to keep practising. I was fond of Sister Ines, despite her appearance. Her skin was grey, she wore thick glasses sitting on a huge nose, and her teeth stuck out so much that she couldn't really close her mouth; but she had a gentle soul. We all thought she looked like a mouse, and some of the naughtiest girls used to creep up behind her and lift her dress to see if she had a tail. Sister Ines of the Order of the Rat, they called her, but to me she was special. She got permission from the Mother Superior to let me practise on the piano in the chapel, and began teaching me the little she knew about musical theory. In the library I found an old book of music, which I studied every night.

Thus it was, in a world of grey habits, a pervading smell of detergent, and the joy of musical scores, that I spent the early years of my life.

Chapter 2

Delos (Greece), 4th century BC

Pyros was walking on the dirt track that led to the top of the hill, not suspecting for a moment how his life would change that day. He was going to give a lecture on astronomy to a group of scholars and was hoping for a lively debate, nothing more. He stopped to savour the view. He had walked this path for years, but the turquoise sea splashing gently onto the white sand still mesmerised him.

***

Pyros was born in 312 BC in Lefkada, an island in the Aegean Sea. His father was a famous mathematician and his mother an Egyptian slave who, having cured her master after a poisonous snake bite that should have killed him, won his gratitude and then his love.

Pyros grew up among quadrants and medicinal herbs, surrounded by the beauty of the island, learning from his father the harmonious arrangement of the universe and from his mother the mysteries of nature.

Lefkada was on the route of the spice trade between Asia and the West. The two cultures mixed easily in the island, and Pyros grew up nourished by both. As a child, he was eager to learn and showed a particular interest in science.

When his father could teach him nothing more, Pyros set off on a journey to acquire knowledge, travelling to Babylon, Egypt, India, Central Asia and beyond. Everywhere he went, his remarkable mind soaked up facts and ideas. He learned that the most advanced societies had knowledge and wisdom at their core.

His passion for science grew stronger, and in his discussions with mathematicians, astronomers and students of nature, Pyros found the answers to many of his questions.

After many years, he returned to Lefkada where he devoted himself to spreading the knowledge he had acquired. A captivating speaker with a rigorous mind, it didn't take him long to find disciples. He endorsed scepticism but on one point he was adamant: knowledge should be accessible to all, rich and poor, slaves and freemen. Mankind couldn't progress if knowledge was reserved for a few.

Following the example of the Egyptians, Pyros established the first public library in Greece. The Houses of Books, as he called them, soon started spreading throughout the Mediterranean. One of their main activities was to transcribe and copy every parchment, so that whenever a new idea was generated, it was quickly shared amongst the Houses. Pyros became one of the best known scholars of his time, and his prestige attracted others from across the ancient world.

That day in Delos, when he got to the House, his audience was already waiting for him. Shortly after he started his lecture, while he was talking about planetary rotation, a stranger joined the group. He had a weather-beaten face and grey hair, and was dressed in a sleeveless white tunic that revealed his muscled arms. In his right hand he held a cane with an ivory top. Pyros was explaining how the Sun rotated around the Earth when the old man interrupted him in a clear and loud voice:

—It is the Earth that rotates around the Sun.

The audience turned around to look at him disapprovingly. Who dared to contradict the great Pyros? For his part, Pyros wasn't bothered at all. He asked the stranger to elaborate.

—The simple explanations are the closest to the truth —the old man said, his voice firm and confident—. If the Sun did rotate around the Earth, the other planets' orbits would be epicycles, quadratics and other very complicated curves. Even the seasons' changes can be better explained if we assume that the Earth rotates around the Sun.

—What are you talking about? —Someone in the audience interrupted—. It is obvious that the Sun rises in the East and disappears in the West. Only if the Sun rotates around the Earth can we explain the movement that we see every day.

—Then, why does the Sun come up and go down at different points on the horizon, depending on the time of the year? —asked the foreigner calmly—. And why do the planets appear in different positions in the sky?

—How do you explain that we can't observe any movement of one star relative to the other? —asked Pyros, genuinely curious and well aware that the calculations made by astronomers were often contradictory—. If the Earth rotated, we would see a different sky every night.

—Because the stars are much farther away than we can imagine and their relative movements can be perceived only with special instruments —replied the foreigner, with a smile that suggested he enjoyed being controversial.

There were murmurs of disapproval from the audience, but the stranger continued.

—You yourself, Pyros, say that we need to be open to new ideas.

—Yes, as far as there are facts to support them — replied Pyros—. What you are saying is a hypothesis that cannot be proven empirically.

The man picked up a bag he had been carrying and brought out a tube with lenses of different sizes. He held it up to show to the audience.

—This instrument allows one to see what the human eye can't reach —he said, passing the tube to Pyros—. Look from the smaller end.

Pyros was surprised how clearly he could see the details of Athene's Temple, more than 20 kilometres away: the shape of the columns; the stairs; he could even see the different types of flowers in the garden. With the scornful muttering continuing in the hall, Pyros looked in amazement through the tube.

—At night you will be able to see better, and you will understand what I am talking about —said the stranger.

—You haven't told me your name and where you come from —said Pyros.

—My name is Elom and I come from a country you have never heard of.

Then, walking towards the door, he turned back, looked at Pyros and said:

—Tonight you can verify what I am saying. I will see you at sunset.

He left the room and the audience buzzed with conversations: who was that lunatic? Where did he really come from? What was in the tube? But Pyros himself wasn't paying attention. He was intrigued by this mysterious tube that somehow shortened distances. After finishing his lecture, he spent the rest of the afternoon trying to understand how it worked.

When the sun started to fade over the horizon, Elom arrived, as he had promised.

—Here you are, Pyros, your curiosity is stronger than your students' prejudices —he said, laying out on the floor several drawings of the Sun, the Earth, the planets and other stars that Pyros didn't recognise.

Elom explained how he had arrived at his theory of the Earth's rotation, the calculations he had made, as well as the new planets and stars he had discovered. Pyros stared at the drawings. If, as Elom said, the stars were so far away, then the universe was much bigger than anybody had ever imagined.

They spent the whole night in deep conversation, using Elom's tube to scan the sky. It was almost dawn, and while Pyros was trying to capture the last gleam of a star, Elom said:

—It is not only about astronomy that I came to talk to you.

Pyros kept his eyes on the sky and replied:

—What do you want to talk about, Elom?

—I have known of you for a long time.

—Am I really known in your land? —asked Pyros, curious.

—Yes, my people do know you. We have been following your progress.

Pyros put down the tube and looked at Elom, startled.

—How do they know me if you tell me that you come from a country that I haven't heard of?

—Listen carefully, Pyros, because what I am about to say will be hard for you to accept, but it will set the whole course of your life —Elom paused—. You are not the same as the rest of the people; your blood-line is different. You are one of us, your destiny is extraordinary and you have a great mission ahead of you.

—I still don't understand you, Elom. I was born from a man and a woman, just like everybody else. I am not different, I can't be different. Besides, I don't believe any mission is more important than the Houses of Books. Don't you agree? —Pyros picked up the tube again, hoping to end this difficult conversation.

—You have seen extraordinary things on your travels —replied Elom calmly—, powerful civilizations that have made progress thanks to knowledge.

—That's exactly what I am trying to achieve with the Houses of Books —Pyros was starting to sound annoyed.

—There is something else you can do.

—What?

—Reality is richer and more extraordinary than you can imagine —said Elom—. The laws that govern the universe are infinitely complex and harmonious.

—I still don't understand what you are saying.

Elom paused for a moment and then continued:

—Your mission is to guide mankind to its enlightened future. Human beings are capable of great ideas and achievements, but they need to be guided, they need to be inspired. Their destiny is to pierce the veil that separates the visible from the invisible, and thus to know the truth about life. You and I, our race of Guides, we facilitate that process. Our work takes many forms, but we work underground and everything we do is anonymous. We are here to inspire generations of men and women to make the necessary changes for mankind to progress. Sometimes our enemies delay us, but they can't stop human progress.

—I think you are starting to talk nonsense.

Elom took some stones from his robe, threw them to the ground and immediately water started to seep up through the earth.

For a few seconds, Pyros was speechless, suspecting a trick.

—Check it yourself —said Elom—. It is water, pure water, and it will turn into a spring and then into a river and people will come looking for relief for their ailments.

Suspiciously, Pyros scooped up a handful of the water that had sprung from the earth, and took a sip. It was water, undoubtedly, but there had never been a spring here before. Elom continued:

—Also, Pyros, you have certain peculiarities. You may already have noticed that you don't age like other people. Some of your younger followers look much older than you do.

Now Pyros was really startled. It was true, he was ageing differently. As he had never paid much attention to it himself, he had put it down to frugal living. But anyway, how could Elom know?

—Even if I wanted to believe what you are saying — Pyros said, visibly angry—, you didn't answer my question. What do you mean when you say I am different? Who are these Guides you talk about, anyway?

—Your blood-line belongs to another race, but it was dormant in your ancestors. There are others like you — other Guides— and in time you will meet them.

—So who are you then?

—I am the Guide of Time —said Elom, his voice quiet and serious—, and your destiny is to become the Guide of your time. That means your mission goes beyond the Houses of Books. The day will come when I will have to leave and you will be my successor, and you will find your successor too.

—I really don't understand what you are saying, and I don't understand what you want from me. I have met many charlatans in my life. Why should you be different?

—This is for real —replied Elom—, just as the water at your feet is real. Your passion for learning and teaching comes from your real essence, what is inside you. It is the inspiration that has guided your steps since you were born. If you weren't so passionate about your beliefs, if your intentions weren't pure, I wouldn't be talking to you.

Pyros was silent for a while. He wasn't sure if he was talking to a skilful lunatic or somebody quite exceptional.

—If I accept what you have said, what should I do about it?

—When you are ready, you will follow me and I will teach you. But I'm not in a hurry, I want you to take your time. For now, you will see life in a different way. Many things will start happening, and you will find new answers to your questions.

—It doesn't sound very convincing.

Elom roared with laughter.

—I know, and I wouldn't have expected anything less from you. Doubt is the main weapon of those who are seeking the truth. Certainty is the enemy of science. As I said: there is no rush, I can wait a few more decades for you. Continue with your life, and over time things will become clear. I will leave the tube with you, and remember it's not only to see the stars. Use it from time to time. You will hear from me soon.

Pyros watched Elom as he walked away through the garden. His silhouette looked as if it was shining with the early light of dawn, and for a moment Pyros thought he was floating. Then he was gone.

Pyros picked up the tube. A blue light was coming from the larger mirror. He hadn't used that end, but when he looked through it, he was shocked. He saw scenes from his past, when he was a child, during his travels, and then other images that seemed to be from his future. He saw himself crossing unknown lands, dressed in strange clothes, in the middle of big cities with unfamiliar buildings. The vision was so intense that he had to look away to stop himself getting dizzy.

Weeks went by without anything special happening, but there wasn't a day when Pyros didn't think of Elom. Three months after their meeting, Pyros had a vivid dream: Elom entered his room, produced a map and pointed at a city on the coast beyond the Aegean Sea. It was called Syracuse, and Pyros had to go there to meet a great mathematician.

Pyros woke up remembering the dream clearly, but he didn't pay much attention to it. During the next two weeks, he kept dreaming of Elom every night, and Syracuse and the mathematician. Then one day, in the wax tablet that he used for taking notes, the map he had been dreaming of appeared. There and then he decided to go to Syracuse.

The journey by boat took several weeks, and Pyros began to feel it was all nonsense. How could he have been fooled into such an adventure? Letting a dream guide him wasn't the way he normally behaved. Then, one morning at dawn, Pyros saw on the horizon the silhouette of a city. It was Syracuse, like a jewel set in an emerald-green bay. With its marble temples and its dense vegetation, it was astonishingly beautiful. He disembarked and walked towards the city, not knowing what to do. As he entered the city wall, he saw Elom.

Pyros hurried over to him, and demanded:

—How did you know I would be here?

Elom gave a friendly laugh.

—I sent you here, don't you remember the dream?

—But...

—Your education has started, Pyros. It's inevitable. The sooner you accept it, the better.

Chapter 3

Bormia (Malta), 20th century

Seeing my progress with the piano, Sister Ines talked to the Mother Superior. An old piano teacher lived in the nearby village, and the nun had persuaded her to give me some free lessons, but, before she could begin, she needed approval. The Mother Superior was initially reluctant, but after Sister Ines claimed it would be good for my soul, she agreed. In return, I had to play the piano in the chapel every Sunday. I also had to help Sister Astencia, who was getting too old to wash the convent's dishes by herself.

Professor Olga —that was what she wanted to be called— was older than Sister Ines, and had a white lock of hair in the middle of her dark black curls. She always wore a long black dress and her face was invariably solemn. The day I met her, she gently pressed my hand without saying a word, then put a piece of paper in front of me. It was covered with lines and squiggles, and I couldn't understand it at all. She stared at me, and I felt quite terrified. Professor Olga smiled sarcastically, took my index finger and put it on the keyboard. "This is G major" she said in the croaky voice of a heavy smoker.

After such an imposing start, things could only get better. Professor Olga came every week for an hour, and always left me with homework that I had to present at the next lesson. She talked very little, but her eyes said everything. If she raised a brow, I knew I had done something wrong. On those occasions she used to take control of the keyboard and say: "This way", and nothing else. Sometimes she looked at me out of the corner of her eye, and over time I came to realise that meant she was happy with me. Despite her intimidating silence, Professor Olga quickly became the most important person in my life, the only one who helped me to see beyond the oppressive grey habits of the nuns, the harsh walls of the orphanage and the aching loneliness that was my constant companion.

One night, as though to celebrate this new turn in my fortunes, Eliza showed up by my bed. She was enthusiastic about my progress with the piano.

—How do you know how I play if you are asleep during the day? —I asked her.

—I can hear you in my sleep —she said with a wicked smile.

Apart from Eliza and the music, life in the convent followed a crushing routine. We woke up at half past four, for Mass at five, prayers at six, breakfast at seven, then lessons until one. Each grade had only one teacher, a nun who taught everything from maths to sewing. The convent was renowned in the area for its delicately embroidered linen, and we devoted the first part of each afternoon to embroidery.

At three o'clock we were allowed out of the classroom and it was then that life really started for me. Rush to the chapel, sit on the bench, open the piano: it was like returning to a treasure chest, an intimate and magical ritual. The piano became my confidant, the exercises were the prayers that allowed me to escape to a world of harmony, and the musical notes were the loving words I craved.

When I turned 12, Eliza came to say goodbye.

—I can go now —she said—, you don't need me any more.

—I do need you!

—Not anymore —Eliza said—. Now you have other things to do and I have to take care of other girls who are lonely. You do understand, don't you?

I looked at her, tears filling my eyes. I hugged her tightly.

—Please, don't go.

—Let's do something —she said—: I will leave, but I promise you that every time you feel lonely, I will come back.

—How will you know when I'm lonely? —I asked, not at all convinced.

—Take this —she said, giving me a black polished rock—. Whenever you want me to visit you, hold it tightly in your hand and think of me. That same night I will come back to the orphanage.

During all the time I was in the orphanage, Eliza came when I called her. I still wasn't sure who she was, but that didn't matter. Perhaps I was imagining her, perhaps she was real. Only many years later did I really understand how extraordinary that friendship was, although strange things kept happening to me as I grew older. I didn't know at the time, of course, but they were the first signs of a life that would be marked by extraordinary events.

Until I was 13, I had little contact with the world outside the convent. Apart from occasional outings to the beach, I used to go on Wednesday afternoons to the village to help Sister Ines with the groceries. Sometimes, when women from the village came to the convent to buy bed linen or table cloths, I helped the nuns. The customers were usually young women who came with their mothers to buy delicate pieces for their trousseau. I looked at their beautiful dresses and high-heeled shoes, their smiling faces, enthusiastically discussing their plans, and I felt empty. I realised I was living in the margins of life, and if I didn't get out of the orphanage soon, nothing would change.

It was then that I started to write a diary. Professor Olga used to lend me books, and once she gave me a copy of "The Diary of a Young Girl" by Anne Frank". The tragic story of the Jewish girl, hiding from the Nazis in her Amsterdam attic, inspired me to write down the emotions that burst inside me, leaving me sleepless as I tried to unravel the confused web of thoughts and anxieties lurking in my teenage mind. But a few months after I started my diary, something quite peculiar happened.

My diary was divided into sections separated by maps of European countries. One day a beautiful blue feather, split at the end into two points, showed up on the page for the United Kingdom, and I used it as a bookmark for my diary. Next day, when I opened the book, the feather was back on the United Kingdom map; and so on for the next few days, even though I put the feather on different pages. I came to the conclusion that one of the nuns was reading my diary. From then on, I limited my entries in the diary to minor events: no more emotions, no more comments about the orphanage or the nuns.

When I turned fifteen, Sister Ines asked the Mother Superior to let me go on my own to the village one Sunday afternoon. To our astonishment, the Mother Superior agreed. I still remember the moment Sister Ines told me the news. I didn't know what to say; I was overwhelmed by a mix of happiness and fear. I had never been away from the orphanage on my own and I didn't know what I would do, but the thought of having a few hours of freedom was exhilarating.

When the big day came, after lunch I went running upstairs to put on a dress that I had made myself and the blue shoes that Sister Ines had lent me; the ones she was wearing when she arrived at the convent more than 20 years earlier. She said goodbye to me at the door of the convent, offering all sorts of advice. I assured her she didn't have to worry and off I went, taking care to turn around and wave to her as I went down the lane. When she couldn't see me any more, I took my shoes off and ran to the village. The air seemed purer outside the walls of the convent and, surrounded by the dark green of the trees and the distant blue of the Mediterranean, I realised I was happy.

That Sunday, a bright sun was warming the air and the only sign that it was the middle of October was a fresh breeze. I came to the outskirts of the village, took a deep breath and started walking down the cobbled streets which ran between the white houses, their balconies full of geraniums in a huge variety of colours. I had walked down those streets before when I went to the market, but this time, they seemed to come alive under my feet. I got to the village square and, with one of the coins that Sister Ines had given me, I bought an ice-cream and sat on a bench.

The scene in front of me was charming. Children were playing, dogs were sniffing around, young couples were idling along, holding hands, women were chatting with their friends. Nobody paid any attention to me, but that didn't bother me at all. If I could be invisible, it meant that I wasn't that different after all, that the reasons why nobody had wanted to adopt me when I was a child had disappeared, and that I was just like everybody else. Without realising it, I spent hours savouring that borrowed happiness.

Eventually I realised I was feeling a bit cold. I looked at the clock in the square: it was almost five, and the light was starting to fade. I jumped from the bench and started running towards the convent. I didn't want to be late back on the very first day of my new freedom. At that time of the year, dusk didn't last long and I soon found myself in near darkness, alone on the deserted road to the convent, hearing only the rhythmic buzz of the nocturnal insects. I was quite close to the convent when I thought I heard steps coming up behind me. My heart started beating faster. Surely I was imagining it: nobody would be on that road at that time of the night.

I stopped briefly, I could definitely hear the steps getting closer and caught a whiff of something that smelled a bit like the wine we used at Mass. I started running again, but the steps still came closer. My blood froze in my veins, and then I heard a man's voice whispering strange coarse words, and I felt his hand on my shoulder. Just when I feared the worst was about to happen, I heard a commotion behind me. I didn't dare to turn around, and ran as fast as I could to the door of the convent. To my great relief, Sister Ines was waiting there, anxiously looking out for me. When she saw me pale and out of breath, she asked me what had happened. Only then did I turn around, in time to glimpse a light that quickly disappeared in the darkness.

Next Wednesday, when I went to the market with Sister Ines, she told me that a criminal had been caught on Sunday evening. He was running through the village, crying for help and screaming that a ghost was following him. The man was wanted by the police for robbery and rape. He didn't put up any resistance when two policemen took him away.

***

One day Professor Olga said she wanted to talk to me and Sister Ines. I didn't know what to expect. Maybe she was tired of me and didn't want to give me lessons anymore. At that time, I was practising six hours a day, but I was never sure if I was doing well or not: my teacher didn't give me many clues.

Professor Olga was waiting for us in the visiting room.

—I think Ariane should apply for this —she said, arching one eyebrow while showing us a newspaper—. The Academy where I studied in London has a programme called Talents in the World. It offers scholarships for foreign students.

I looked at Sister Ines, astonished. She was blushing furiously:

—It is a great opportunity! Thank you so much, Professor Olga.

Then, looking at me, Sister Ines said:

—This is what you were looking for, Ariane, you must take part! I don't swear because it is a sin, but if I could I would swear that our little girl is the perfect candidate for a scholarship. She plays like an angel, isn't that right, Professor Olga? What do we have to do?

Sister Ines and Professor Olga started a complicated conversation that mostly went over my head, but one thing I did understand: Professor Olga thought I was good enough to apply for a scholarship, and that was the greatest compliment.

The two women decided to fill in the form and post it off straightaway. After that there was silence, and I began to lose heart. I shouldn't have been so impatient because a month later, Professor Olga showed me a letter.

—Read it —she said. Unusually, the white lock in her hair was out of place, as if she had been rushing.

I cried out:

—I have been accepted for an audition!

Sister Ines squealed with delight, and her teeth stuck out even more than usual. She started pouring with sweat and stuttering:

—Aaa...riane, my sweet girl, ththth... is your opportunity. God is opening the doors for a future beyond these four walls. You will win a scholarship, I am sure!

—I don't want to disappoint you but now comes the really difficult part —Professor Olga said—. You have to practise a lot, I mean a lot, Ariane, and I mean a lot. You have to play until your fingers bleed. Do you know how many students will apply all around the world? Hundreds, perhaps thousands! I will give you lessons twice a week from now on, but you will have to work harder.

—When do we start? —I asked.

Professor Olga quickly became more tyrannical than usual. She laid out a programme of practice that challenged the strict rules of the chapel's schedule —and at times, my health as well. The wooden rule she used to keep the rhythm seemed to fall closer and closer to my fingers. During our marathon lessons, she wouldn't let me stand up to stretch, not even for a few minutes.

—If you want to win the scholarship, you have to work harder —she said arching her eyebrow.

Sometimes, during the long hours of practice, Sister Ines brought me tea and biscuits and stayed with me, her expression one of delight, bordering on ecstasy. At night, while the others were asleep, she would take me to the chapel so that I could carry on practising. If we were caught, she told me, she would claim it was her fault. Running from one octave to the next, I repeated arpeggios, quadruplets and trilling notes. The rickety old metronome didn't stop: tic, tac, tic, tac.

—Play in your head, my sweet girl. Imagine the music in your mind, and even when you are not practising, play an imaginary piano.

The pace of work was overwhelming, and of course I also had to carry on with my duties in the convent. One day while I was cleaning the kitchen floor, I mistakenly put oil instead of chlorine in the water. The Mother Superior was furious, but she calmed down after Sister Ines's explanation:

—The girl is a little bit blind —she said, and then she crossed herself in apology for her pity lie.

Professor Olga suggested that we didn't mention anything to the Mother Superior about the scholarship.

—I know the Mother Superior —she said—. It is better that she doesn't find out. If she does, for every minute you spend at the piano she will demand something from you in return.

Looking back now, I realise I never thanked Professor Olga enough for all her support during those long months. Two weeks before my audition, Sister Ines and Professor Olga started planning the details of our trip. They briefly discussed who should come with me on the journey and, because they couldn't agree, they asked me whom I would prefer. I looked at Sister Ines and her sweet mouse-like face, and said in a low voice "Sister Ines". I thought Professor Olga would be very upset at me but, to my surprise, she patted my head tenderly and said:

—I would have chosen her too.

As the days went by, Sister Ines became more and more nervous. One night I woke up with a start, hearing her heavy breathing by my bed. The moon was shining through the dormitory window, and I could see tears in her eyes as she whispered:

—Oh, Ariane, my sweet girl. I will miss you so much!

She was just as lonely as I was, but at least I was 16 and could dream of a world outside the convent. She was going to be there, alone, for the rest of her life.

I read as much as I could about the United Kingdom and what I found out was fascinating. At the same time, Sister Ines doubled her prayer-time with her favourite rosary. It was a sin to call it a good-luck charm, she told me, but every time she used it, her wishes seemed to come true.

—Ora et Labora —she said in Latin—. Pray and work.

At last, the great day arrived. It was a Monday, and Sister Ines and I hadn't slept at all. The bus to Valletta —where the audition would take place— took about two hours along a rough road. To make sure we wouldn't miss my audition at 10, we would catch the first bus, at six in the morning. It was still dark when we left the convent, and I had never seen such a starry sky; even the vibrant smell of the dew seemed full of promise.

We were the first to get to the bus stop, but we were soon joined by a few people from the village who commuted every day to the capital. A recent storm had caused landslides along the road, so the journey of two hours actually turned into three hours. The bus had to find its way around puddles, piles of mud and broken-down cars until at last we arrived in Valletta. We were still in time, but only just.

I had never been to Valletta before, and I was astonished by the traffic and the noise. Even so, it seemed like the sky was brighter and the sea bluer. I felt a new sense of excitement, but at the same time what lay ahead made me increasingly nervous. What would the examiners be like? Would other students be there for the audition?

After getting lost several times, we arrived at the address we had been given. When I saw the place, I felt my heart shrinking: it was a luxury hotel, several storeys high and with a lobby of shiny granite. Outside, a porter in an elegant blue coat smiled at us and asked if we wanted to go in. Sister Ines stuttered a few words, saying we were there for an audition. The man looked surprised, but he opened the door. We were overwhelmed by the whirlwind of smartly-dressed men and women, smiling staff and suitcases so big that all the dresses in the convent would have fitted into just a couple of them.

Another man in uniform noticed our confusion and asked us if we needed help. Sister Ines, trying to recover her composure, managed to produce the letter inviting me to the audition. What the man said left us stunned: we were in the wrong place! No auditions were taking place in the hotel. Sister Ines's stutter got worse:

—Itifit's not popossible.

I started to feel faint, but at that moment something unusual happened. A man with grey hair and a kind smile was just walking past and spotted the letter with the Academy logo that Sister Ines was holding. He asked us if we were going to the audition. Sister Ines and I looked at him, but we were still so shocked that neither of us could answer. The man in uniform intervened and said yes, we were looking for the audition, but we were in the wrong place. After a brief exchange between the two, the man told us:

—It is your lucky day. My name is Christopher Grace and I am the director of the Academy programme. I sent that invitation and that's my signature. I am on my way to the auditions now; if you want, you can come with me.

From that day onwards, Mr Grace became my guardian angel; the flesh and blood version, anyway.

Chapter 4

Syracuse, 3rd century BC

For weeks now Archimedes had barely slept. He hadn't even had a bath. His faithful slave, Demetrius, had never seen him so withdrawn and distant. He knew that when his master had a problem to solve, he isolated himself in his world of pulleys, cylinders and spheres, but this time was different. He seemed obsessed. He made designs on the scrolls piled up on his work desk, on the ashes in the fireplace or even on his lap as he sat, head bowed and silent.

Demetrius was the son of a slave of Phidias, the famous astronomer and Archimedes's father. As children, he and Archimedes had been inseparable, but before long, their interests grew apart. Young Archimedes was always submerged in complicated calculations, and at night he often spent hours staring at the sky with his father. He looked so vulnerable that Demetrius felt that he would need to do more than look after him. He would protect him, and never leave him alone.

So Demetrius went with Archimedes on all his trips. He stayed with him when he went to study in Alexandria with the greatest mathematicians of the time. He admired Archimedes unconditionally. In his eyes, he was much better, much cleverer than all the other scientists. Conon and Eratosthenes, both friends of Archimedes, didn't have his intelligence and originality; but they were happy to benefit from his brain. Demetrius used to get very upset when he found out that others had taken credit for ideas that Archimedes innocently shared with them, something that happened several times.

Back in Syracuse, Archimedes's reputation flourished, not only because of his knowledge of mathematics but, above all, for his inventions. Syracuse's tyrannical ruler, King Hiero, was a distant relative of Archimedes and when he became aware of his distant cousin's genius, he commissioned him to take on all sort of projects —not only for his military campaigns, but also for his personal whim. To Archimedes, engineering as a discipline was inferior to mathematics; but, partly to please the temperamental king and partly because he found the challenge entertaining, he worked on any assignment Hiero gave him.

So Archimedes built a boat that could be used for different purposes: for luxury trips, to deliver supplies or as a war ship.

When the Siracusia set sail for the first time, it had on board six hundred people, a garden, a gym and a temple to the goddess Aphrodite. It was the biggest boat that had ever sailed in the Mediterranean up to that moment. Archimedes supervised its construction down to the tiniest detail.

To be able to pump the water up from the bilge, he put a propeller-shaped metal sheet inside an inclined cylinder. The movement of the propeller would lift the water from the bilge to the deck. The device was so successful that later it was used to carry water from distant rivers to irrigate the thirsty fields that fed the people of Syracuse.

Hiero ordered his creative cousin to invent devices to repel the continuous assaults of the Roman forces. The first one was the Claw, a large wooden arm from which hung an enormous metal hook. When the hook was dropped on an enemy boat, its weight sank the foredeck so that water could get into the ship. And when the hook was quickly lifted, the boat was already listing and soon it sank.

Archimedes's reputation spread around the Mediterranean. To his fellow citizens he was a genius and a saviour, and he was feared and respected by his enemies. For those who didn't know him well, it was hard to believe that the man who walked through the streets of Syracuse, his hair uncombed and his clothes torn and dirty, was a brilliant mathematician and an expert in the art of war. Demetrius knew better, and he also knew how to interpret what was occupying his master's mind. He made sure that no mundane worries bothered Archimedes, so he could concentrate only on surprising the world with his inventions.

One of Archimedes's most renowned moments came when Hiero —perhaps wanting to ridicule his relative who was becoming too popular amongst the citizens of Syracuse— asked him to demonstrate his theory about the infinite possibilities of the lever.

—Give me the place to stand —Archimedes used to say—, and I shall move the Earth. Challenging Archimedes to prove that claim, Hiero asked him to move a very heavy object.

Archimedes chose a boat that was in dry-dock, and also asked it to be loaded with people and supplies for a long trip. The ship was so big that a dozen people couldn't move it even when it was empty, but Archimedes, with a system of interconnected pulleys that worked as a lever, pulled a rope and slowly moved the ship and its heavy load out of the dock and down into the sea. Hiero had to admit that his cousin had a superior mind. In the eyes of the people of Syracuse, Archimedes had become a demi-God.

One day, the king asked him to solve a problem that seemed simple but which puzzled Archimedes for months. Hiero gave a well-known goldsmith a large bar of gold to make into a crown worthy of a king. The goldsmith did a wonderful job and created a fine piece of art: "Worthy of a great monarch", he said to Hiero. But the king wasn't convinced that the crown was made of pure gold. He suspected the goldsmith had mixed in another metal when casting the crown, so he asked Archimedes to find out the truth.

The first idea that Archimedes had was to melt the crown, the quickest way to find out what it was made of. Hiero refused to do this, as he didn't want to lose his beautiful treasure. So Archimedes tried to solve the problem mathematically. He tried measuring its sections, approximating each to a solid shape whose volume could be estimated; but the cumulative errors made the estimate too imprecise. To test if the crown was made of pure gold, he needed to know its density; if the goldsmith had used silver or nickel, its density would be lower. But the formula to estimate density required two values: volume and weight. The weight was easy, but how could he measure the volume of such an irregular object as a crown? Week after week, the solution eluded him.

One morning, Demetrius woke his master up with some news that he thought might lift his spirits.

—Why are you waking me up so early? —asked Archimedes, half asleep.

—Master, it's almost midday and two foreigners coming from Alexandria are here to give you news of Conon and Eratosthenes.

Archimedes sat up, excited at the thought of hearing from his friends. Demetrius helped him out of bed, dressed him and went with him downstairs where the visitors were waiting.

Archimedes looked at them. The younger one had a familiar face, but he couldn't remember where he had seen him before. Maybe during one of his trips to Egypt. He would ask Demetrius later, surely he remembered him.

—Welcome to my home. My servant says you have news from Alexandria.

—That's right, Archimedes, we come from Egypt where we spoke to your teachers and your friends. You left a powerful legacy at the school there and your reputation as a great inventor has spread throughout the Mediterranean.

—Really? —asked Archimedes, distracted—. Do you have news of Eratosthenes and Conon?

—Your friends are doing well —said the eldest with a smile—. Eratosthenes is now in charge of the library in

Alexandria and is still busy with his many interests. He is a respected astronomer and has expanded on Dicearco's calculations for measuring the Earth's dimensions. He keeps writing poetry too.

—Wonderful! What can you tell me about Conon?

—He continues with his studies about the eclipses and is writing the fourth volume of De astrologia. Both send their regards and want to know when you will visit them. They have sent you some papers that they thought might interest you.

—Let me see —said Archimedes, taking the papyrus the foreigner produced—. You have made me realise how much I miss Alexandria. Once I finish the king's assignment, I will go and visit them.

Then, turning to Demetrius, he said:

—Prepare a room for our guests.

—We are grateful for your hospitality, Archimedes. We will stay only a couple of nights —said the eldest, handing his few bits of luggage to Demetrius—. If you will allow me, can I ask what is the king's assignment?

—Are you interested in finding out the volume of irregular objects? —asked Archimedes.

—It interests me a lot.

They talked for a while about the calculus of density, inevitably without reaching a conclusion.

Then Demetrius entered the room:

—Will you forgive me, noble foreigners, the master has a commitment in the city.

—It's true. I forgot. I have to go —said Archimedes briskly, turning his back on his guests. As much as he enjoyed the conversation, he wanted to be alone to think about the issue at hand. The trip to the bath would give him that opportunity.

Archimedes left his house thinking about density, volumes and irregular shapes. Suddenly he remembered he hadn't asked the foreigners their names, but then his mind turned back to the puzzle of the crown. He was making his way to the public baths, because Demetrius had at last persuaded him to have a proper bath, which would also help him to relax. When he got to the bath-house, the slaves undressed him and took him to a private section where there was a big marble bath. Demetrius always reserved it for Archimedes, so nobody could bother him. It was the only way his master would stay long enough in the water to make up for the infrequency of his visits.

Archimedes lowered himself into the steamy and perfumed water that covered him up to his neck, and a slave massaged him with jasmine oil. He closed his eyes feeling his body sliding into a comfortable torpor. His mind relaxed, and he was almost sure he could hear a gentle music in the background. He saw an image of the younger man who had just visited him, and sunk his head under the water. As he did so, he heard water sloshing out of the bath and onto the floor.

It came to him in a flash: he had found the solution! He jumped out of the bath and forgetting to put his clothes on he ran out into the streets of Syracuse yelling: "Eureka, I found it!".

When he got home, naked and wet, Demetrius thought that this time his master had really gone crazy.

—The water —shouted Archimedes—, it was so easy...the volume... it's the same as the water that's spilled!

—Master, what's happening? You need to calm down, let me put a robe around you.

Archimedes ran from one corner of the house to the other, waving his arms in the air, looking frantically for his papyrus and talking to himself. Demetrius managed to wrap a towel around him and dried him as best he could while his master was sketching mathematical diagrams in the air.

—Maybe you need to sleep, why don't you try? — Demetrius said, seriously worried.

—Are you insane? At last I have solved the problem. The volume of an object submerged in the water is the same as the volume of displaced water! It was so easy! Now I can find what the king is looking for. Bring me a large bowl of water and send a message to Hiero. By the time he receives it, I will know the truth about the crown.

—I will, master, but what will happen if you need me? I don't want to leave you while you are in this state.

—I feel better than ever. I won't need you, the other slaves can serve me. Besides, the foreigners are here too.

—No, they left.

Archimedes looked disappointed.

—But they said they would stay a couple of days.

—Yes, but they're gone —said Demetrius

—Did they say anything?

—Yes, actually. When they left, they said they had already achieved what they came to do.

Perplexed by the foreigners' words, Archimedes said:

—I don't even know their names.

—Pyros and Elom, master.

Chapter 5

Twenty miles underground, on New Year's Eve 1999

Alexander came out of his deep meditation and opened his eyes. He was celebrating his birthday surrounded by his closest friends, in one of his favourite places. Even the Seers were there. They were all sitting in silence, celebrating the occasion. Every year at this time, he received guidance from his masters, which helped him to see clearly the path ahead of him, what to expect in the near future. But, this time was different. Instead of the sense of peace that he usually felt, he was anxious. His visions told him that difficult times lay ahead.

The visions the Seers had shared with him flashed across his mind, so vivid he could almost touch them. Again, the conclusion was clear: there would be wars, tensions and continuing ignorance in many parts of the human world. A new threat was growing. It looked like the most challenging he had ever known. As the Seers showed him the images of the future, one face in particular was quite distinctive. Although the Seers didn't let him see what role this character would play, Alexander recognised the face. It had featured in his dreams throughout his life. Now, he realised, he would soon be meeting its owner.

Alexander shivered. All the Guides had a mystery to solve at some stage in their existence, and success meant they could move to higher planes of learning and guiding. Alexander's mystery was obvious: he had to figure out that face.

***

On the same day, on the surface in Siberia, Zardoff was leaning against a snow-sprinkled tree deep in the forest. He was finishing his meal: the heart of a bear he had killed with his own hands. It was his favourite dish, and part of the enjoyment was the ferocious struggle he always had with the animal. But on this occasion, Zardoff wasn't enjoying himself as much as usual. He was struggling with a familiar feeling. However much he wanted to break all his ties with the Guides, he could still perceive that something was going on in the Caves, something that would have a significant impact on him, that would put him in danger.

Many times he thought he had defeated the Guides for ever, that he had eliminated their power and influence. But, much like weeds, they always seemed to grow back.

In one sense only, Alexander and Zardoff shared a view of the future. Both knew that there were difficult times ahead. Their destinies were tied in a way Zardoff didn't understand, but he knew that a new and powerful threat was looming. This would be the most important battle of his life, and he could sense that Alexander felt the same way.

Once Zardoff had finished eating, he started his journey back. The dogs that pulled his sledge obeyed his orders instantly. They were terrified of him. That was Zardoff's way, to dominate and control, to inspire fear. He smiled grimly to himself, knowing that terror had been successful over many centuries. It would be again, he was sure of that.

Chapter 6

Bormia (Malta), 21st century

The journey in the taxi was short and nobody said a word. Sister Ines was sweating under her old habit and I could barely control my nerves. Only Mr Grace seemed calm, and from time to time he looked at me and smiled. When we arrived at the place where the auditions would take place, the Malta Academy of Music, we followed him to a room in the basement and he asked us to wait. There were other girls and boys in the room, and when Sister Ines and I came in, they all turned to look at us; some of the kids didn't even try to hide a mocking smile. We sat in a corner, terrified.

After a short while, a young woman came in to tell us the auditions would take place in two different rooms, one for theory and the other for the recital. Each session would last an hour. I didn't have to wait long, as my surname was one of the first on the list. Sister Ines and I went into a room where we were greeted by Mr Grace, who introduced us to a woman with short hair, small glasses and bright eyes. Her name was Carol Hobbs.

—Welcome Ariane —she said in a soft voice—. Christopher told me he found you in the wrong place.

—That's right, Miss Hobbs —I managed to mumble.

—Call me Carol, please. We were lucky he found you —she smiled—. Sister Ines, you are Ariane's guardian, is that right?

—Yeeeesss —she answered, her face red.

—Fine, if you wish to stay, please have a seat in one of the chairs by the wall.

—Ththtththanks.

Then, turning to me, Carol said:

—I see you have been studying with Professor Olga Del Monte, a distinguished graduate of the Academy —said Carol.

I moved my head slightly.

—We saw her last night. She is a good friend of mine —intervened Mr Grace—, and we were students together at the Academy. Please sit at the piano. You chose three pieces. Could you please start with For Elise by Beethoven?

I sat at the piano and my hands started sweating. For a moment I had an irrelevant thought: what if Sister Ines's sweat was contagious? I rubbed my hands on my skirt, took a deep breath and put my fingers on the keys. They were smoother and whiter than the ones on the convent piano, the white and black of the keys in sharper contrast, and they made a much more refined sound. After a brief stumble at the beginning, I took another deep breath and soon I felt I was flying away, to a place where the notes seemed to dance in the air and time stood still.

When I finished, I looked up and saw Carol's smiling face and Mr Grace's shining eyes.

—Well done, Ariane! —she said—. The beginning was a bit shaky, but then you started to transmit your feeling very well.

I didn't know what to say, but I felt myself blushing.

—Please, continue with the first movement of Liszt's Sonata in B minor —said Mr Grace.

Calmer now, I started playing and at the end their applause was reassuring. Mr Grace then asked me to play Concert No. 3 in D minor by Rachmaninov. When I finished, I looked at Sister Ines and cringed when I saw she was dribbling, as she often did when I was practising. Carol and Mr Grace talked quietly to each other for a moment and then, with a big smile, he said:

—Well done, Ariane. Wait outside, please. We will be making a decision today.

Out of the room, Sister Ines gave me a big hug:

—Today you have played better than ever, my sweet girl. The scholarship is yours, I promise you.

We went back to the waiting room and sat down. I could see Sister Ines moving her hand in the pocket where she kept her miraculous rosary. It was the first time I had had that type of test, and the experience had left me quite confused. On the one hand, I felt great satisfaction; on the other, terrible uncertainty. Then the time came for the theory test, with a Mr Siegren and a Mrs Horton as the examiners. They asked questions that I didn't know how to answer, which made me tense. At the end they didn't say anything, and I knew they were not impressed.

After a few hours, during which we were offered sandwiches, juices and tea, only one other girl and I were left in the room. Sister Ines had drowsed off when Carol and Mr Grace finally came in.

—Ariane, please, come back to the recital room —said Carol—. We would like you to repeat the Rachmaninov piece you have chosen in front of our colleagues.

Mr Siegren and Mrs Horton were waiting inside. When I finished playing, I looked up and all four of them seemed hypnotised.

—Wonderful, Ariane! —exclaimed Mrs Horton.

They turned their back to me and started whispering, and occasionally Mr Grace looked around with a reassuring smile.

After what seemed like an age, it was Mr Grace who spoke:

—You have done very well, Ariane. Congratulations. You have impressed us with your skills and the emotion of your performance. Olga taught you well. You have some gaps in theory, but nothing serious, so we have all decided you will have the scholarship.

I gasped, not believing what I had heard, and Sister Ines's mousy face started to turn purple while she waved her arms in the air. For a moment it seemed she was choking, so I patted her firmly on the back. When she managed to recover her breath, yelled:

—You made it! Yes, you did, my sweet girl! —And she hugged me so tightly that I ended up with bruises on my arms.

It was true. I had won the scholarship! Something inside me spun around and made me lightheaded, as if my body knew that my whole life had changed in that single moment.

Carol, much amused, interrupted us:

—You have to be in London by mid-September at the latest, and in our experience, it's never too early to start sorting out the papers. Ariane, do you have a passport?

Sister Ines's expression answered the question. Carol said:

—You must have a passport to get into Britain, so Sister Ines will have to make this a priority. The scholarship will also cover the trip to London and all living expenses. It is not a huge amount of money, but it will be enough to live. If you could send her some extra money, Sister Ines, that would be ideal.

Sister Ines, face still puce, said:

—This poor girl doesn't have anybody in this world except us, the nuns, and we have made a vow to be poor, and the convent doesn't have any money to spare. We barely survive. It will be very difficult to send her money.

—Don't worry, we will find other ways to top up the scholarship. For now we need to make sure the paperwork gets done. Do you know where to start?

—No... but don't worry, we will manage. Ariane will be in London on time for the beginning of the course.

As we were about to leave, Mr Grace congratulated me and with a big smile said:

—You will do really well in England. I can promise you that.

Getting the passport and sorting out other documents proved more daunting than I expected. Being an orphan was hard emotionally, of course, but I soon discovered that even the simplest bureaucratic procedures were doubly complicated for me. Because I was a minor, I needed permission from my parents or guardians to travel, but the nuns had never formalised their role as my guardians. In bureaucratic terms, I didn't exist in my country; I was an unknown citizen. Sister Ines and I spent entire days running from one place to the other, filling in forms, taking them to the local government offices, but each time the officials kept asking for different things.

Carol called us every fortnight to ask how things were progressing, and it was thanks to those conversations that I began to understand what "English phlegm" meant. While Sister Ines seemed on the verge of a nervous breakdown, Carol remained calm and insisted we shouldn't worry. Other candidates had gone through the same process; in the end, they always got the documents they needed.

On one occasion, when it seemed that a magistrate was about to prevent my departure, Carol intervened and told us she would talk to the Maltese Embassy in London. We never knew what she did, but in less than three weeks I had my passport, a permit to travel, a birth certificate, a good conduct recommendation and a Single Status certificate, just in case.

The night before I was due to leave, Sister Ines became very emotional. She kept taking off her glasses and drying her tears, and she was breathing heavily through her swollen nose.

—I am going to miss you so much, my sweet girl —she said, hugging me hard till I could hardly breathe.

—And I will miss you too, Sister.

—You are going to be a great pianist and you will make all of us in the convent very proud. And maybe one day you will take the decision …

—I will think about it, Sister Ines —I interrupted her—, but for the time being I just want to go to London to study music.

—Yes, Ariane, I know. I am not the one who is pushing this, I was just told to remind you.

I knew perfectly well what Sister Ines was talking about. Since I was a child, when it became clear that nobody would adopt me, the Mother Superior had often told me how wonderful it was to devote one's life to the Lord. Being Jesus's wife was the highest aspiration of any woman and would make me immensely happy. If I decided to become a nun and stay in the convent, I would be doing God's will, she said.

The Mother Superior, Sister Ignacia, wasn't the most inspiring person herself. For a start, her looks were against her: she had thick black eyebrows, a menacing expression and her upper lip was unmistakably hairy. Sister Ines once mischievously told me she was sure the Mother Superior shaved. Yet what really bothered me was her breath: onions were part of our daily diet but she ate them like fruit. They affected not only her breath but her clothes too, and forever after I associated religion with the smell of onions. Besides, I had no intention of becoming a nun, trapped in the physical and emotional chains of religion. The further I could get from the convent, the better it would be for me.

Chapter 7

Louyang (China), 2nd century AD

—The Divine Consort will receive you briefly —said a servant, bowing before putting a golden tray with a cup of tea on a lacquered table in the middle of the room.

Cai Lun was waiting impatiently for Deng Sui, the consort of the late Emperor He in the antechamber of the audience room. Cai Lun had been there several times before and knew it well: the armchair covered with silk and the beautiful wall tapestry depicting the story of the Han dynasty. Cai Lun smiled to himself, remembering the first time he had been in this room, when he was one of the eunuchs in the court and the Emperor had called for him asking for advice on a dispute between concubines.

He had come a long way since then. Thanks to his wisdom and his skill in navigating through the many palace intrigues, Cai Lun became one of the Emperor's trusted advisers. In due course, the Emperor put him in charge of developing new weapons, a crucial role in the court.

When Emperor He died, his favourite concubine, Deng Sui, took charge of the throne while his son, the official successor, was still growing up. Deng Sui was a wise woman, intelligent and with principles —more than the

Emperor had, thought Cai Lun—, but her position in the court had been continually undermined.

Yin, the Emperor's first wife and holder of the title of Empress, had always been jealous of Deng Sui. She made no secret of her goal: once the Emperor died, she would get rid of the concubine and her family. The ambitious Deng Sui decided to set a trap to discredit her. Thanks to Cai Lun's political cunning —he had helped Emperor He's mother in similar circumstances— it didn't take long to spread a rumour that the Empress and her brothers were practising witchcraft against the Emperor and his concubines. Emperor He, always very superstitious, believed the rumours and banished Empress Yin and her family in disgrace. Devastated, the Empress had to leave the palace immediately, and a few days later she committed suicide. Her brothers and sons were sent into exile, leaving Deng Sui free to take control.

When the Emperor died, Deng Sui replaced him on the throne and Cai Lun became her closest ally and Imperial Adviser. Even though the intrigues in the palace continued and Yin's sons didn't stop plotting from their exile, Deng Sui was a clever and skilful ruler and Cai Lun was happy to help her.

On that particular day, though, Cai Lun didn't want to be waiting on Deng Sui. He had more important issues on his mind. In his role designing new weapons, he was in charge of several workshops for experimenting and innovation, but the project that was dearest to him actually had nothing to do with war. To consolidate her power, Deng Sui had asked Cai Lun to find a new way to reproduce official documents.

Silk was too expensive and bamboo too heavy; Deng Sui wanted her orders to reach every corner of China in less time and at a lower cost. If an alternative could be found, it would allow all the silk in China to be used for commercial purposes, and that would generate more income for the imperial funds. Cai Lun's workshops had been trying different materials and techniques for copying but they still hadn't found the right mixture. Then something Cai Lun saw that morning had given him new hope.

He was a devout Buddhist and, just as he did every morning, he woke up early and went to the temple. At the entrance he saw a man writing on a thin, rough sheet that Cai Lun had never seen before. It was neither silk nor bamboo, but it looked light and the letters could be clearly seen. From the colour of his skin and the shape of his eyes, the man looked as if he were from the Far West, thought Cai Lun. He came closer and stretched out his hand to touch the sheet. With a mischievous smile, the man said he could have it if he wanted it.

Cai Lun was amazed to hear the foreigner speak his language, but he was more interested in the sheet. Where did he get it? The man told him that he had bought several sheets from nomads in the Hindu valley, who used it to store food. Cai Lun thanked him for the gift, and asked the man to stay at his home for a couple of days so they could talk more about this discovery.

While they were on their way back to Cai Lun's house, a messenger stopped them to say that the Empress needed to see Cai Lun urgently. Irritated by the interruption,

Cai Lun decided to go home first with the foreigner to make sure he didn't lose him.

—I don't know your name —said Cai Lun—, nor where you come from. How did you learn our language?

—My name is Pyros, noble Cai Lun. I come from the lands beyond the great mountains, beyond the great deserts. I learned your language during my travels through your beautiful country.

—What is your occupation? —asked Cai Lun, intrigued.

—I am a philosopher and an educator. I travel to learn and spread knowledge.

Now Cai Lun felt even more frustrated to have to interrupt this conversation with such an interesting visitor because of Deng Sui's whims.

A few minutes later they reached Cai Lun's home, an elegant wooden building with a pyramid-shaped roof. Two servants were waiting with bowls of water, silk kimonos and slippers.

—Welcome to my home, Pyros. Come in, please.

Beyond the entrance wall there was a large room, with a round panelled ceiling supported by golden columns at each corner of a squared drawing on the floor. The structure had a religious meaning: the rounded roof was Heaven, and the square was the Earth. A bright-green dragon, with rubies in its eyes and a large white pearl in its mouth, hung from the centre of the ceiling. Below the dragon was a round table and on it, a delicate porcelain vase full of flowers. In the reception room there were several large sofas and beautifully carved tables, and the floor was covered with carpets. The effect was majestic, worthy of an Imperial Adviser.

From the room they went to Cai Lun's study, its walls lined with books. In the middle was a desk made of mulberry wood and an armchair of red silk. In contrast with the reception room, the study was rather sober.

—You must be tired. Can I offer you a cup of tea? — said Cai Lun, while inviting him to sit down.

—I would appreciate it.

Cai Lun ordered a slave to take care of his guest while he was away at the palace, and, whispering into his ear, he told him that on no account was he to let the visitor leave.

Cai Lun walked out of his house and into a sedan chair. He ordered the four carriers to take him first to the workshop where he showed the master craftsman the mysterious sheet. They discussed what it might be made of and decided to tear off a small piece for a thorough inspection. Cai Lun then went on to the palace.

After waiting in the anteroom for half an hour, he was relieved when the consort came into the chamber. Cai Lun bowed and, after a gesture from her, they sat down. Cai Lun kept his eyes down, as imperial protocol required, looking at her feet until she snapped her fingers signalling he could look at her.

Deng Sui went straight to the point:

—The tribes of Qyiang region are arming themselves for war, and Yin's brothers are behind it. We must hurry to spread our messages across the empire. How is the project going? Why it is taking so long to find a new material?

—We are spending many hours on it —he said—. But you are right, Divine Consort, it has taken time to find the right material, though now I think we are on the right track.

—I am glad to hear that. We need to be vigilant. Our enemies will never leave us in peace, so we need to make sure all our subjects receive our orders.

—Yes, Sublime Deng Sui. I hope I will be able to give you good news very soon.

—Before coming to this meeting —said the consort— I was told you met a foreigner this morning who had a sheet of a material nobody had seen before.

Cai Lun wasn't surprised. Even though he was one of her closest allies, Deng Sui never really trusted anybody, and he had always suspected she was spying on him. That comment just confirmed it.

—That's right, Chosen One. I was intrigued by the material the man was writing on; I took it to the workshop to identify what it is made of.

—I shall be informed every day on this matter. We want our orders to get out to the provinces as quickly as possible.

—I am at your command; I will keep you informed personally.

—I know I can trust you. Tomorrow we will be waiting for news —she said smiling at him before she left the room.

The Empress was getting impatient, concluded Cai Lun. He had to work faster.

He asked the carriers to run to his house. When he went inside, he looked for Pyros.

—I am sorry I left in such a hurry this morning —said Cai Lun—. The Empress already knows about the sheets you brought and she is very interested. But it is almost lunch time, so please join me and we can continue talking.

While lunch was being served, Cai Lun kept up a stream of questions:

—What do you know about the nomads who sold you the sheet? What do they live off? What type of trees and flowers grow in that area?

Pyros talked about his trip to the Hindu Valley and described the area in detail. "The foreigner is an unusual character" —thought Cai Lun—. "Not only does he speak our language, but he seems to know a lot about many different subjects."

After lunch, Cai Lun went to his rooms for his afternoon rest, telling Pyros that they would go later to the workshop. A slave helped him undress and put on his afternoon silk robe. Cai Lun lay on the soft mattress of goose feathers and put his head on a perfumed pillow. He closed his eyes, hearing soft music that lulled him into a deep sleep. In his dreams he saw exotic forests and strange animals and, beside a river, a young man with straight black hair and dark skin holding a wooden bowl. He was mixing water with scraps of cloths, bark, fishing net and hemp leaves. Behind the young man, hanging from a branch of a large tree, there were several sheets similar to the one his guest had given him in the morning. The young man stood up, took one of the sheets and with an inky finger he wrote the words: Cai Lun.

Startled, Cai Lun woke up, soaked in sweat. He called out to his servant and dressed quickly. He needed to talk to Pyros, but he wasn't in his bedroom. They searched the house but couldn't find him. Perhaps he had gone out for a walk, Cai Lun thought, so he decided to go to the workshop on his own. He ordered the craftsmen to start preparing the mixture he had seen in his dream. He stayed there throughout the night waiting for the results, and just before dawn, one of the sheets looked remarkably like the one Pyros had given him. Cai Lun asked for a pen and black ink, and wrote his name. The ink dried, and the words didn't smudge. Cai Lun had found what he was looking for.

Thanks to this discovery, Cai Lun became a very rich man and got an aristocratic title. Paper became widely used in China, allowing the consort to centralize her power, but it also helped to spread literacy and the development of Chinese literature. By the seventh century, China's papermaking method had reached Korea, Vietnam and Japan. In the 9th century, some Chinese papermakers were captured by Arabs and paper spread to the Middle East. It was not until the 12th century that paper was introduced to Europe. It revolutionised written communications and provided a platform from which human civilisation would change for ever.

Chapter 8

Bormia (Malta) 20th century

There were only a few days left before my departure and I sat in the dormitory that had been my home for as long as I could remember, looking out of the window. The sun seemed to be stretching itself across the distant sea so as not to let it go. Before I had the chance of going to England, I used to imagine what was beyond the blue line of the horizon: fantasy places, luminous cities, people I might one day meet. But it had never been more than a dream. Now, as it was actually starting to come true, I felt dizzy, my nerves chewing away my stomach.

It wasn't only the uncertainty of what was waiting on the other side, new people, a new country; the embarrassing truth was that I was terrified by the thought of flying. I couldn't understand how such a heavy object could leave the ground, let alone fly. Sister Ines knew about my anxieties and she tried to calm me down:

—Don't be afraid, my sweet girl. People who know about it say that flying is not dangerous. Apparently we are more likely to die slipping in a bath than on a plane.

—Yes, I've heard that, but how do they fly? —I insisted.

—That I don't know, but there are a lot of clever people who are quite happy flying. Professor Olga's husband used to fly all the time and she went with him often.

That was what she said to me, but once I overheard her talking to another nun:

—My poor sweet girl. It must be awful to be locked in a metal cage at 10,000 metres. How can such a heavy thing stay up?

The day before my departure, the nuns organised a farewell supper and invited some people from the village too. I sat next to Sister Ines and Professor Olga, and before the blessing of the food, I took their hands to thank them for what they had done for me. Mother Superior said a few words about how proud the community was of my achievement. Then she sank her teeth into a turkey leg, which kept her busy for the rest of the evening.

Next day I woke up early. We had to leave for the airport at 10, but I wanted one last chance to see the places where I had lived all my life. I went to the chapel and knelt down automatically. Suddenly I realised I would never be forced to attend Mass again: what a wonderful thought! I caressed the piano, opened it and played a few notes. I was going to miss my old friend. I breathed in the chapel's familiar air, charged with humidity, incense and candles, and I said goodbye.

I walked through the corridors, remembering how many times I had longed for somebody to take me away from there. If I had been adopted, would I have had the opportunity to go to London? Maybe not. Maybe all my lonely years at the convent would one day prove to have been the better way.

At nine o'clock I was ready. Sister Ines had given me her old suitcase, and I had packed two pairs of trousers, a couple of shirts, sweaters and a coat that Professor Olga had bought me in a second-hand shop. Sister Ines had arranged a taxi to take us to the airport, and she held my hand throughout the journey.

—Promise me you will take care of yourself and eat properly —she said tearfully—. You need to take medicines and buy some warm clothes. English weather can make you ill.

—Don't worry, Sister Ines. I will be careful with the weather —I stroked her hand.

—And the food. It's very bad; they eat only fish and chips. You have to eat lots of fruit and vegetables, otherwise you will get ill. They don't have the sunshine we have here, and that's why English people are sad all the time.

I smiled. Subconsciously, Sister Ines, who had done so much to get me out of the convent, was trying to discourage me from leaving.

Our farewell was very sad. My dear Sister Ines was convulsed in sobs, as if a fountain of tears repressed for years had finally found a way out. I felt guilty about leaving her alone.

— Oh, my dear Ariane. I will miss you so much. My only consolation is that I know this is what you want, this is your chance to be free and happy.

—I will miss you too, Sister Ines, I will write every week and call you as often as I can, I promise.

Then, taking my hands, she said:

—I will tell you something you don't know. The day you arrived at the orphanage, you were the prettiest thing I had seen in my life, but Mother Superior didn't want you to stay because we didn't have enough space. I prayed very hard with my miraculous rosary, asking our Lord to let you stay. A few days later, a couple came to the convent and adopted three girls at once. That had never happened before, and it meant that Mother Superior didn't have any more excuses to get rid of you. You are the answer to my prayers, Ariane, the way God winked at me, telling me that He listens to me. And the truth is, my sweet girl, I don't know what I would have done without you.

I hugged her tight until the final call for my flight. I turned around to wave one last goodbye; then, seized by both fear and excitement, I walked away from the only life I had known.

The next few minutes passed in a blur. I found my seat by the window, thinking that everyone else was much calmer. My hands started sweating and I didn't know what to do with the straps on my seat. At that point, a young man sat down beside me. He had warm brown eyes and he smiled, asking me if I wanted some help. He fastened my belt and introduced himself as John. He told me he was actually a pilot himself.

Before long the plane started shaking, and making a thunderous noise. I grabbed the seat arms, and John smiled again and said quite calmly:

—Don't be afraid. Air travel is very safe.

—But the noise …

—That's normal, the engines will be running at full speed while we take off. When we stop climbing, you will hear just a purr, nothing more.

Instinctively I closed my eyes, still terrified, but John talked quietly about the training that pilots received, how planes were built, how they are maintained, how the plane we were travelling in was one of the safest. His voice calmed me down. An hour into our flight, we were given some food. More food, in fact, than in my three daily meals at the orphanage. John asked me the reason for my trip. He seemed very impressed that I was a pianist and was going to study at the London Academy of Music. He congratulated me, saying I had to be very good to get in there. I turned my attention to an exquisite chocolate pudding and started watching a movie, on a small screen in front of me. Half way through the story, and by then completely relaxed, I fell asleep.

When I woke up, John passed me an orange juice and some sweet bread.

—You looked so peaceful that the flight attendant didn't want to wake you up —he smiled—, but I did keep your afternoon snack.

I was surprised that I was already hungry again. It must have been the altitude. Soon I realised that the plane was pointing down, we had gone through the clouds and I could see green fields and houses down below.

—We are about to land —said John—. Is anybody going to meet you?

—Yes, a lady from the Academy will be waiting for me.

As we left the plane, John said he was going to hurry ahead. He shook my hand, and gave me a small card.

—If ever you are in trouble, give me a call.

The card told me that his full name was John Andrews and he lived somewhere called Winchester. To my surprise, in one corner of the card there was a drawing of a two-pointed blue feather with the spot in the middle, very much like the one I had found in my diary. I looked round to say goodbye, but he had already gone.

Chapter 9

Ujjain (India), 7th century AD

As he did every afternoon, before spending long hours staring at the vastness of the sky, Brahmagupta went to the temple at the Ujjain astronomic observatory to light some incense and pray. The temple was small and on the altar was an image of the God Shiva, fresh yellow flowers and a painting of Ganesha, the elephant-God. The smell of incense filled the room, and the scientist thanked Shiva for his good karma, his family and his successful career.

Winters in Ujjain were cold, especially at night, and they bothered Brahmagupta more every year. His joints were painful, distracting him from his prayers. He covered his shoulders with the Kashmir wool shawl that his wife had knitted for him, and continued with his prayers.

When he had finished he went to his study. It was cluttered with maps, books and leather folders, leaving only enough room for a small prayer mat. The roof was a stone-made vault, open to the stars. The observatory had been built more than a thousand years ago, and in many ancient maps it was shown as the first meridian. Many famous astronomers, mathematicians and even poets had studied there, and Brahmagupta was immensely proud to have been chosen to run it.

The astronomer wasn't always easy to deal with. He didn't hesitate to criticise those scientists whose ideas he thought were undignified or who contradicted the sacred Hindu texts. To Brahmagupta, the perfect order of the universe was more evidence of Brahma's infinite power, and that rigid attitude had won him many enemies. Brahmagupta had written a book, About the Right and Established Doctrine of Brahma, where he explained in detail his astronomical discoveries and how these confirmed the Vedas, Hinduism's holiest script. In it, he criticised fiercely those who disagreed with his theories.

As was the norm amongst astronomers at the time, he wrote in verse, giving a flowery touch to descriptions of planets, equations, geometric figures and even his enemies.

Brahmagupta had a remarkable record of predicting solar eclipses and planet movements, and that day in particular was an important one for him; he would know if his estimate of the time when Saturn would appear in the horizon was right. He waited calmly, looking at the sky, and Saturn appeared precisely when he thought it would.

Elated by his success, Brahmagupta let his mind wander to another topic, one that had intrigued and perplexed him for years: the use of zero. Most scientist saw zero as a simple placeholder, a symbol that didn't have any role in mathematics. To Brahmagupta, though, that didn't make any sense. What he was searching for was a set of rules that would define zero in a way that was consistent with the widely-agreed calculus.

He was scribbling some verses about his thoughts when a servant came in with a cup of tea and ghee, and told him that an emissary from King Khosrow II of Persia wanted to see him.

Brahmagupta was surprised; he wasn't expecting anybody, least of all at that time of the night. But he was pleased by the news. He had close relations with Persian scientists, and he often got together with them to exchange their latest findings. He asked the servant to show the visitor in, and a few minutes later he was greeting a man with fair skin and grey hair. The stranger was around 50, and though he had a westerner's features, he was dressed as a Persian, with an amamah on his head, a heavy tunic and leather sandals.

—Great Brahmagupta, I hope that my unexpected visit doesn't bother you.

—Persian scholars are always welcome.

Brahmagupta invited him to sit down, as the man carefully put his sack full of maps and books in a corner. The servant brought him a cup of tea.

—Thank you for receiving me —the stranger said— especially at this time of the night. I have a very important message and I must return immediately to the king's palace.

—Tell me your name, and what I can do for you —said Brahmagupta.

—My name is Pyros, wise master. I am King Khosrow II's scientific adviser. The situation in Persia is getting more critical every day. The king is facing rebellions in his own ranks, and Constantinople is a constant threat. He doesn't know how long he will be able to resist, which is why he sent me to give you some manuscripts produced by the court's mathematicians.

—I am very sorry to hear about the king's troubles — replied Brahmagupta sadly—. I knew the country was going through difficult times, but I didn't imagine they were so serious. Even more reason to welcome you. The king has done a lot to strengthen the ties with India and the exchange of knowledge between our countries.

Pyros kept talking while he laid out some of the manuscripts he had brought with him. To Brahmagupta's surprise, one of them showed an image identical to the symbol he was using for his own calculations: a circle surrounded by elliptical orbits.

—Our scientists have been trying to develop the rules for zero —Pyros spoke quietly, his words carrying great authority—. It's a well-known concept of course, but only you have approached it in the right way. Unlike other mathematicians, you don't look at numbers as simple tools to count and measure. Your approach is the same as our scientists'. They treat numbers as abstract entities, with precise rules that allow scientists to work out solutions to mathematical problems.

—That's exactly what I think! —Brahmagupta couldn't keep the excitement from his voice.

Pyros continued:

—For the zero to have a reason to exist, it needs to be used as a number and not merely as a symbol without any value. In the opinion of the Persian mathematicians, many calculations don't make sense unless they take account of the series before the zero.

—Negative numbers, as debts —interrupted Brahmagupta, hardly daring to believe how similar their thoughts had been.

—Yes, negative numbers, as debts —answered Pyros with a smile—. The king was right; you are the best person to spread the wisdom of our scientists.

—I am honoured by the king's faith in me. Please stay in the observatory for as long as you need and we must talk some more. I will give instructions for you to have a room and you can use the library whenever you want.

—Thank you, Brahmagupta, but I really have to go back to Persia to support the king.

—Then it is time to say goodbye, Pyros. Please send my regards to the king, with my sincere wishes that his troubles will be over soon.

Pyros bowed briefly and was gone. Brahmagupta decided it was time to go home. The conversation had left him worried about the king's problems, but also astonished at the similarities between his and the Persian thinking on zero.

The night air cleared his head and Brahmagupta looked up: he had never seen such a starry sky and he thanked God for its beauty. He walked slowly towards his home, seeing his wife's silhouette in the doorway. She was holding an oil lamp to guide his path. That sight comforted him every night: there was Prama, there was home.

It had been a good idea to marry her. She was seven years younger than him, faithful, a devoted wife and they had had four children together. Prama was a quiet woman, and Brahmagupta sometimes wandered what she was thinking behind that sweet and melancholic smile. Maybe she missed her land at the foot of the great mountains. When their parents arranged their marriage, Brahmagupta was so busy with his studies that he didn't meet Prama until their wedding. She was just fourteen, barely more than a child, with dark and scared eyes. It took them a long time to consummate their marriage; they didn't know what to do, and anyway Brahmagupta was working day and night. Right from the start, Prama had taken to waiting for him with an oil lamp, a cup of tea and a blanket to warm him up after his long nights watching the sky.

Before reaching his house, Brahmagupta looked up once more. To his delight, a shower of shooting stars was crossing the sky at precisely that moment. What a sight! Shooting stars meant good fortune; to Brahmagupta, they were Divinity expressing itself in all its glory. Prama watched him, wondering what was still grabbing his attention after so many hours looking at the sky in the observatory. But she didn't ask; she was used to his spending more time with his eyes on the sky than on Earth. When the star showers ended, Brahmagupta went inside, drank tea, wrapped the blanket around him and went to his bedroom. Prama helped him undress and put on his night gown; he blew out the lamp and quickly fell into a deep sleep, dreaming of stars.

The next day, Brahmagupta woke up earlier than usual and decided to pray to the domestic gods. He walked out of the room quietly to avoid disturbing Prama, lit some incense and started his meditation. Usually he found it easy to empty his mind and connect with his spirit, but this time he struggled. Numbers, planets and stars danced in his imagination and then a zero with elliptic orbits, just like the one Pyros had showed him a few hours ago. All of a sudden, as if in a flash of light, some strange verses came to his mind:

The sum of two positives is positive,

of two negatives negative.

The sum of a positive and a negative is their difference;

If they are equal it is zero.

The sum of a negative and zero is negative,

that of a positive and zero positive,

and that of two zeros zero.

A negative minus zero is negative,

a positive minus zero positive;

zero minus zero is zero.

As though in a trance, Brahmagupta went to his study to write the verses down. By mid-morning, he had defined the rules for the use of zero, opening a new era for mathematics and science.

Later in his life, Brahmagupta found a solution to the general linear equation and made significant contributions to algebra, trigonometry and geometry. His work was so widely acclaimed that his contemporaries called him the Jewel of Mathematics.

Chapter 10

London, 21st century

All the luggage on the conveyor belt at London airport seemed modern and shiny, and I immediately recognised Sister Ines's battered old case. As I walked nervously towards the exit, I could see smiling faces, names on boards, flowers and even some balloons. And I could see Carol. What a relief: she hadn't abandoned me. She waved, and gave me a warm smile.

—Welcome to England —she said, getting a sweater out of her bag—. Put this on, we don't want you catching a cold the first day you are here.

The journey into London was surreal: the traffic seemed like a metal river moving slowly through the rain.

—London's traffic can be quite slow —said Carol apologetically— especially when it's raining.

—Sister Ines says that the rain means good luck —I replied.

—Then you will be very lucky in England —Carol laughed.

During the journey, she told me when I was going to start the lessons, where I was going to live and all about my landlady.

Elspeth Bowman was the widow of a British diplomat, and had lived in many exotic countries. She spoke several languages, so when her husband died, she decided to rent rooms in her home to foreign students. I would stay with her for the first few months and then, if I wanted, I could move.

—But Elspeth is charming, you won't want to leave — said Carol—. At the beginning you will have to work harder than the other students, because you need to catch up with the theory. But don't worry, it will be easy for you.

Carol's enthusiasm and confidence encouraged me.

—I can't wait to get going —I replied.

—Next Monday, first thing in the morning, you will start your lessons. In this folder you'll find all the information you need to get to the Academy. I will meet you and introduce you to the teachers.

By the time we reached the centre of London, the sky had cleared and timid rays of sun were setting over the city. Carol decided to take a detour to show me Parliament Square and the House of Commons, the seat of the British Parliament. The neo-gothic building on the border of the river, its towers stretched towards the sky, was breathtakingly beautiful. A Union Jack waved majestically from the top of the building and I felt strangely happy; the flag seemed to be welcoming me to the country.

Of course, I immediately recognised Big Ben, the most common picture in the books I had read about England. We drove past Westminster Abbey, where royal weddings were celebrated and which housed the tombs of some of the most illustrious names in history. Artists, politicians, scientists —buried there to keep alive the pride of a country in its fascinating past. I was mesmerised: how magnificent everything was compared with the squalid place I had lived in.

A few minutes later, Carol stopped the car in a quiet street and rang the bell at number 29. A small, slim woman with piercing blue eyes opened the door. She was Mrs Bowman. Looking at me with a nice smile, she said:

—Welcome to my home, Ariane, I hope your stay will be comfortable. Come in, please, and take your shoes off. At my age it is not so easy to keep the floor clean.

—Maybe I should go now Mrs Bowman —said Carol—, it's getting late and I don't want to trouble you.

—That's fine, Carol, thank you for bringing Ariane here.

Before leaving, Carol shook my hand, and with her warmest smile said:

—Goodbye then, I will see you on Monday, Ariane. I am sure you will settle in quickly.

—Thank you for everything, Carol. I can't wait for Monday. I'm so excited!

—Now, you do need to eat something —said Mrs Bowman when Carol left—. It is a bit late for tea, but we can't waste some treats I've prepared. Come to the kitchen, please.

I looked around at my new home. Every room was crammed with furniture, ornaments, paintings and carpets, and it seemed to welcome me. The kitchen too was full of pots and pans. In one corner was a table with a teapot and some cakes that looked and smelled delicious.

—Do you know about scones? They are typically British, the best companion for a cup of tea, especially if you add jam and cream.

—Thank you, Mrs Bowman, you shouldn't have bothered.

—I don't think you eat enough —she said, looking me up and down.

—Maybe —I replied, busy trying a scone.

—Carol told me you come from Malta, but you look more North European to me. I have had students from many parts of the world and I've learned how to guess from their looks and accents where they come from. You're a tricky one, I can't quite place you.

While she was talking, a second scone was melting in my mouth, along with the cream and jam.

—This is quite delicious, Mrs Bowman.

We talked for a while in the kitchen and then I washed up our cups and plates, despite Mrs Bowman's protests.

—Let me show you your room, dear. It's in the attic, but you have the best view. The stairs are narrow and steep, and the carpet is quite tired, so be careful.

We climbed two floors to my room at the top of the house. It was small and warm like the rest of the house, and compared with my dorm in the convent, it was pure luxury. The bed was made of light wood, and covered with a white duvet with pale blue and yellow flowers; there was a bedside table with a pretty lamp, a wardrobe, a desk, and a vase of flowers with a note: 'Welcome to England'. Off the bedroom was a tiny lavatory and a basin; to have a shower or a bath, I had to go to the bathroom downstairs. My room was cluttered with pictures and small ornaments, and the carpet was faded. I didn't care: to have a room of my own was thrilling.

—Your window looks down on the garden where I plant vegetables; you never know when there might be a famine —said Mrs Bowman —. From here you can also see Hyde Park. I must take you there one day.

—What a view! And the room is so welcoming and warm —I said—. Thank you Mrs Bowman!

—Since my husband died, I have rented it to foreign students. It was his study, where he read his books and listened to his music. Now, Ariane, listen carefully. There are two rules in this house: smoking and talking about politics are both forbidden. Fifty three years living with a smoking diplomat was quite enough for my lungs and ears.

—Fine, Mrs Bowman —I replied, laughing.

—If you want a bath or just to rest for a while, dinner will be ready in an hour. I will see you in the kitchen.

—Thank you so much, Mrs Bowman.

I unpacked my clothes and went to the bathroom. I was used to having a cold and quick shower in the orphanage —the nuns gave us only a few minutes to wash. But in Mrs

Bowman's bathroom there was no sign of a shower. In the middle of the tiny room there was a big bath. I didn't like the thought of submerging myself in cold water, so with great relief I realised that one of the taps was for hot water. I filled the bath and climbed in, sinking slowly up to my neck. It was as if every cell in my body was relaxing, and I nearly fell asleep. When I got out, I felt that the water had washed away a thin film of dust from the orphanage and, with it, my former life.

When I got down to the kitchen, dinner was ready. While we ate, Mrs Bowman told me that before getting married she had been a teacher in one of the most famous private schools in England, and had even taught one of the princesses. After describing the girl's none-too-regal behaviour, she started talking about the weather: a favourite topic of conversation among the British, she told me, laughing.

After dinner, she showed me round the house, picking up photo-frames and pointing to her daughter Emily and her husband Harry with the granddaughter, Helena. She showed me a photo of her late husband, Lawrence, a handsome man with an infectious smile. At the end of the tour, she took me down to the basement, where to my surprise she had a large store of food, bottled water, torches, candles and medicines.

—You never know when something terrible might happen —she said, mysteriously.

At nine thirty I was ready to go to bed and her 'Goodnight, my love' sounded like a caress. I went to my room, put on my old pyjamas and snuggled under my warm duvet. I had always suffered from insomnia in the orphanage and I had hoped that it would change when I left; but the past twenty-four hours had already transformed my life and I was too excited to sleep. Carol, Mrs Bowman, London. The images went round and round in my head.

I heard some steps outside my room and I realised that the lights were on; maybe it was Mrs Bowman. I opened the door, but nobody was there, and to my astonishment, I found on the floor a beautiful blue two-pointed feather with a silver dot. What was a feather doing outside of my door? Maybe the same birds that visited the orphanage also lived in Mrs Bowman's roof. I was puzzled, but when I went back to bed I fell asleep immediately.

Chapter 11

Gall, (Switzerland) 9th century AD

Sebastian's parents didn't oppose his wish to become a monk; in fact, the Count and Countess of Villeneuve were quite pleased. Except for the first son, young men in conventional families had only two options: the Church or the army, and Sebastian had never shown any interest in war. He learned how to read when he was a little boy and he always had a book in his hands. Quiet and withdrawn, a monastery would be the perfect home for him. Sebastian joined Saint Gall's Abbey in the year 850 AD.

The Abbey was founded in 747 AD by Charles Martel, Baron of the Franks, next to the grave of Saint Gall, a hermit monk. Twenty years later, Pepin the Short, son of Martel, set up a library as a centre for study and research. Art, science and philosophy flourished. The monks' task was to copy books and manuscripts from all over the world. The Abbey became one of the most important centres of knowledge in Europe.

Sebastian adapted quickly to the monastic life. Thanks to a generous donation from his father, he was given the role of the library's curator, his ideal job. None of the monks knew he was an atheist —he wouldn't have been admitted if they had— and he dutifully attended all the religious services. Actually, his mind was busy reviewing what he had learned in the library. Whenever he had even a minute of free time, he spent it reading.

As curator, the young monk met the leading philosophers and scientists of his time. His distant manner seemed to mellow when he was with visitors, and it was hard for him to break off these conversations to fulfil his religious duties. His favourite books were on science —geometry, mathematics, medicine and botany. He studied them, transcribed them, and treated them with a reverence he didn't feel towards the cup from which he drank wine every morning at Mass.

One day he was summoned to see the Abbott, an elderly man who reminded Sebastian of a little bird. He found him talking to a foreigner. Sebastian bowed to show his respect.

—May God bless you, son —said the Abbott.

—Amen —replied Sebastian.

—You are the library curator, son? —asked the Abbott kindly.

—Yes, Father.

—Our visitor, the philosopher Pyros, has been a friend of the Abbey for a long time. Thanks to him, we have got several invaluable manuscripts. Now he is asking for help from us, and we want to return the favour. You are the right person to support him.

—What can I do for you? —asked Sebastian.

—I would like to investigate some of the plants in this region.

—We have several books on the subject. Do you have any particular manuscript in mind?

—I am looking for a treatise on medicinal plants. I am trying to compile a record of all herbs with healing powers.

—I don't remember seeing that treatise, but of course I will help you look for it.

—We can start now, if that's possible for you —said Pyros.

—Yes... I suppose so —answered Sebastian.

Taking leave of the Abbott, they went to the library. At that time of the day there were a couple of monks reading in silence. Pyros inhaled deeply:

—There is nothing like the smell of books —he said to his young companion.

Sebastian didn't reply, but he thought the same. To him, there was nothing like going every morning to the library and embracing the smell of paper, leather and ink that came off its shelves.

—I will start looking for the document you need —said Sebastian.

—I know where it is —said Pyros.

—I don't think you will, we have just reorganised the sections and changed the positions of most of the documents.

—I know, but if you look for a scroll written by Pedanius Dioscorides on the fourth shelf of this section —said Pyros, pointing at one of the shelves—, you will find it.

Sebastian looked at him with scepticism, but went to the shelf. It didn't take him long to find a manuscript bound in sheep leather called De materia medica whose author was, indeed, Pedanius Dioscorides. The text had a series of drawings of flowers and plants with detailed explanations of their use.

A small smile played on Pyros's face as he carefully put the book on a table.

—You can stay as long as you want —said Sebastian.

—Thank you.

Pyros asked for two more titles, and Sebastian left him, obviously at home amongst books and scrolls. Sebastian was still puzzled —how did the foreigner know where Dioscorides's book was? But it was already midday and he had his religious duties to attend to: the Angelus, and — after a light lunch— afternoon prayers.

When Sebastian returned to the library, Pyros was still there, deep in his books.

At five pm, Sebastian told him:

—We have to leave, I'm afraid. The library isn't open during the evening.

—That's fine, I have taken enough notes for one day.

—Do you have a place to stay?

—Yes, don't worry —said Pyros—. The Abbot told me where to go. See you tomorrow and thank you for everything, Sebastian.

Pyros came back to the library every day for a month. Sebastian didn't know where he spent the night or where he ate, but his energy seemed unlimited. He arrived in the morning with a bunch of herbs that he had collected earlier, spent all day reading and taking notes, and left only when the library was about to close.

One afternoon, while he was copying an Assyrian scroll, Sebastian thought he smelled burning. He looked up in horror to see an oil lamp overturned and a pile of paper on fire. Sebastian didn't have time to react before Pyros put his hands on the flames and snuffed them out completely. For a moment, the young monk thought he was hallucinating, but no, there was a small mound of ashes and Pyros standing over them.

Calmly, Pyros said:

—I had to put the fire out quickly. We don't want to lose any of these extraordinary books.

—How did you do that? —Sebastian asked in astonishment.

—One day I will explain, but for now I want you to know that you can do the same.

—What do you mean?

Pyros didn't answer and continued classifying herbs.

—Can you please explain what just happened? — insisted Sebastian.

—Don't be impatient, Sebastian. This is not the right time —answered Pyros, with a calm smile.

Several weeks went by, but Sebastian couldn't get the fire incident out of his mind. One evening, as the library was closing, Pyros asked him to meet in the morning to collect some herbs. Sebastian made sure he was outside the library in plenty of time, and Pyros arrived promptly at 6 am. They headed for the forest near the Abbey, in thick early-morning mist. Pyros seemed to know where he wanted to go, and an hour later they arrived in the forest.

They sat down on the damp grass and Pyros took a scroll from his coat. It looked familiar to Sebastian.

—Is this yours? —asked Pyros.

—It's not mine. I don't know what you are talking about —Sebastian felt very uncomfortable.

—You wrote it. Go on, please, open it.

Sebastian unrolled the scroll, getting paler as he did so.

—How come…?

—How come I have your scroll?

—Yes… no…

—You are afraid that the Abbott will find out.

—I…

—Don't be, your ideas are not crazy, Sebastian. They are irreverent —heretical, our dear Abbot would say—, but not crazy. In fact, I agree with most of what you say.

—I don't know what you are talking about —replied Sebastian, trying to regain control of himself.

—You don't need to deny it, I know it's yours —said Pyros, amused—. I have been following you for some time. Do you remember when I said you could put the fire out? That's true, Sebastian. You can do that and much more.

—I don't understand what are you talking about; maybe we should go back.

—You know there is something inside of you, something that distinguishes you from other people. If you want to, you can become a sage, a man who would guide others.

Sebastian looked at Pyros as if he were a lunatic, but he was very intrigued: first the fire, and now Pyros had his scroll. How did he get it? Sebastian had hidden it in a box in the library that nobody else had access to.

—You are wondering how I got your scroll? In the same way that I put the fire out. Have you ever asked yourself, Sebastian, why you have premonitory dreams, or why sometimes you know what other people are thinking?

Sebastian was silent for a while, still worried that Pyros could denounce him to the Abbott. Eventually he looked up at Pyros, shrugged his shoulders and said:

—What do I have to do?

—Just give me a few hours every day, and then you can decide what you want to do.

Sebastian, still uncomfortable and suspicious, shrugged again:

—All right, I will do as you say.

***

The next few months were the best of his life. He learned from Pyros a new science, fascinating and mysterious, and, to Pyros, Sebastian was the perfect disciple: obedient and inquisitive, intelligent and persistent. The more he learned, the more he was excited by the possibilities he could imagine ahead.

A year later, Sebastian decided to leave the Abbey, never to return. He travelled with Pyros in different countries, and eventually they went to Kievan Rus' (1) where they met Alexander.

(1)A federation of East Slavic tribes in Europe from the late 9th to the mid-13th century, including parts of modern Belarus, Ukraine, and Russia.

Chapter 12

London, 21st century

Mrs Bowman knocked at my door and came in with a cup of tea.

—I hope you don't mind me waking you up, but I forgot to mention last night that I have to go to the market. I thought you might want to join me, so you can start getting to know London.

I was surprised how much I had slept. In the convent I used to wake up at five every day. Not even on Sundays were we allowed to stay in bed so late. I dressed quickly, but as I rushed out of the room, I tripped and fell down the stairs. When I sat up, a little face with blonde hair and blue eyes was peering at me through thick glasses. I recognised her from the photos and smiles, but she looked scared and ran away. When Mrs Bowman saw me on the floor, she bent down to help me to sit down on the sofa. She then produced a first aid kit that she kept down the stairs in case of accidents. I was amazed to see all the instruments and medicines she kept in there. She told me that, apart from being a teacher, she was a trained nurse. Once she seemed to be reassured, she let me stand up.

In the meantime, the little girl had been looking at the scene. She introduced her: she was indeed Helena, her granddaughter, and was going to spend the rest of the day with us. Emily, Helena's mother, left her once a week with Mrs Bowman and the visit to the market was a ritual. After a quick breakfast, Mrs Bowman, Helena and I went out.

The cold slipped under my clothes and I soon started shivering. Mrs Bowman, by contrast, thought the day was 'beautiful'. When we got to the market, I was amazed: meat, fish, vegetables, fruit, clothes and books —the stalls went on and on and Mrs Bowman knew them all. Helena was obviously delighted as well, especially when her grandmother let her choose some food for lunch. In the middle of the crowd, I noticed a man who seemed to be staring at me. He was tall and heavily built, his face by turns serious and cruel. I was going to say something to Mrs Bowman, but when I turned round again, he had disappeared.

When we returned home, Helena asked lots of questions about lunch. She liked cooking and wanted to help her granny with the food. I had had only a cup of tea and some fruit for breakfast, so I was pleased to see that Mrs Bowman had already prepared a Shepherd's pie that she put in the oven and in few minutes a mouth-watering smell was filling the kitchen.

We sat down at the table, and by now Helena had got over her shyness. She asked me many things fixing me with the same quizzical expression she had when she saw me trip on the stairs. While we were eating, a black cat with white paws came into the room meowing, rubbed against my legs and jumped on my lap.

—Pepe! —cried Mrs Bowman.

In the orphanage, I always had longed for a pet so I was sorry when Mrs Bowman picked the cat up and shut it in the utility room. She told me she had found Pepe ill and malnourished in the streets in a town in Spain, and had saved him from some little boys who were throwing stones. To bring it back to England, she had to arrange for Pepe to get vaccinations and a passport. I said I had been through a similar process, and Helena laughed at the idea.

We finished lunch with a slice of juicy blueberry tart and a cup of tea. I still remember every moment of that lunch with Mrs Bowman and Helena. It was the first time I had had an idea of what a home would feel like, even if it was a borrowed one. Then I remembered Sister Ines and I wished she were there with me, I felt guilty that I was enjoying all this warmth without her. I helped Mrs Bowman to wash the dishes and went back to my room to read the folder that Carol had lent to me, and then at around four I heard a light knock on the door. It was Helena coming to say goodbye, as her mother had arrived to pick her up.

I went down to the kitchen and found Mrs Bowman reading a book. She offered me another slice of pie, saying she was determined I put on some weight. She suggested we go for a walk, and before I had time to protest, she handed me a warm coat.

We left the house and walked towards the Academy. Twenty minutes later I saw a beautiful building like a temple illuminated with lights from the ground. I could hardly believe it: this is where I would spend the next two years of my life. I was astonished by it; everything about it was inspiring, and I, a little girl from an orphanage, would be there. When we got home, a man was waiting for us at the front door. It was Christopher Grace.

—Good evening, Elspeth. Ariane, I can see you are already dressed for the English weather.

—Good evening, and come in, Christopher —said Mrs Bowman, opening the door—. We have just been to see the Academy.

—I was in the neighbourhood and stopped by to see how Ariane is settling in. I will stay only a few minutes, I don't want to disturb you.

—I am fine, Mr Grace —I replied—. Mrs Bowman has made me feel very welcome.

I was touched by his kindness. Now I had two people whom I barely knew taking a real interest in me.

—Are you going to stand outside, Christopher? Do come in and have a cup of tea —said Mrs Bowman.

—I don't want to bother you, Elspeth.

—Oh, you don't bother me at all! Sit down and talk to Ariane while I make some tea.

Mr Grace wanted to know about my journey and my first impressions of London. When I said that the only thing I didn't like was the cold, he laughed and assured me he would solve the problem that same week. Next Saturday, somebody from the Academy would take me out to buy some warm clothes. Mr Grace drank his tea, exchanged a few words with Mrs Bowman and said it was time to go. At the door, he added:

—I am really pleased you have come to England, Ariane. Your talent is very rare. Let's make the most of it.

I was surprised and flattered by his words. When I went back to the kitchen, Mrs Bowman was obviously excited. Even as a young woman she had known of Mr Grace. He had gone on to become one of the most famous conductors in England, and he was still busy supporting various music organisations and charities.

—He is still attractive—she said, with a shine in her eyes.

I was starting to feel hungry. I was amazed by my appetite since I'd left the convent. Mrs Bowman explained that all the students who came from warmer countries got very hungry when they arrived in England. That was why the body accumulated fat, to protect itself from the cold. Because I was so skinny, she thought, my body would be getting even hungrier. She warmed up some potatoes, cauliflowers and mince, and we sat down.

During dinner, she kept talking about Mr Grace and also gave me some advice on how to be safe in London. It was a big city and anything could happen, she said. After doing the washing-up, I went upstairs. I was so tired that I fell asleep immediately.

Like the night before, the noise of footsteps on the landing outside my room woke me up. I looked at my watch: it was only 4 am. The steps stopped by my door, and then I saw a bright light shining through the keyhole. I rubbed my eyes, thinking I must be dreaming, and when I opened them again, the light was gone. I went back to sleep, puzzled and a little troubled. At 7 am, the alarm woke me up.

Chapter 13

Corfu, 12th century AD

In a corner of the room, in a leather armchair too big for his fragile, old body, Pyros was sleeping in front of the fire. His modest house was cluttered with books, papyrus and magnifying glasses, and nothing else. The only real ornament was a beautiful water pipe, crafted from silver and lapis-lazuli which was Pyros's favourite stone. Timo, his faithful servant, came in from time to time to bank up the fire and make sure his master was warm.

They had met in Paestum, a Greek city in the south of Italy, around 60 BC —it was so many years ago that Timo didn't remember the exact date. He was a shy little boy with big sad eyes, and lived in Apollo's temple. The priest allowed him to stay there as long as he kept the temple clean and the oil lamps lit day and night. After his duties, Timo went every morning to the House of Books where he sat for hours behind the bookcases listening to the wise men who went there to teach. One day he learned that the founder of the Houses of Books was going to Paestum to give some lessons in astronomy, and he managed to get into the lecture room. Whilst Pyros, the great Greek master, was talking, a papyrus fell off the table and rolled towards Timo. The little boy picked it up carefully and cleaned it with his tunic. He handed it to the master with shaky hands, and

Pyros asked him his name. He didn't answer: Timo was mute.

Pyros took him on as his helper, and Timo started a long and fascinating journey in his service. Together they visited strange countries, crossed oceans to discover unknown civilizations, and met people who changed history. They witnessed the rise and fall of the Roman Empire, the birth of new religions, the wars between them, and much more.

Undoubtedly their happiest times were during the rule of the Abbasids in Persia in the 8th and 9th centuries. Science, culture and religion flourished harmoniously, and the words of wise men were valued as highly as the blood of war heroes. The Abbasid caliph expanded the Persian Empire and trade prospered. Islam flourished like never before.

With the support of the local rulers, wherever Pyros and Timo went they founded new libraries and centres of study. Young people, both men and women, were taught by the great sage. Timo came to know all his master's disciples, particularly Alexander, who later became Pyros's successor. He was devastated by the loss of Sebastian and was by Pyros's side throughout his struggles with Zardoff. But this particular night in Corfu, where they had moved for Pyros to spend the last years of his life, when Timo saw his master sleeping by the fire so frail and peaceful, he had to accept that Pyros's time was up. He had to get everything ready for his master's final journey.

The imminent arrival of the Arcane was announced by the usual signs: birds flying away, a mild earthquake and the penetrating smell of an electric storm.

When the Arcane eventually appeared, he found Pyros resting in his bed:

—At last! You have arrived! —Pyros greeted him.

The Arcane answered him with his indecipherable smile:

—I am sorry for the delay. You were needed here a bit longer, but now the time has come. Are you ready?

—I have been ready for many years. Alexander is well prepared to be my successor.

—Yes —replied the Arcane, his tone laconic.

—He has been the best of my students.

—Zardoff was good too.

—I know —said Pyros with a sigh—, he was, and he has now completely blinded Sebastian.

—He is very dangerous. Zardoff never came to terms with the fact that you didn't choose him. He will do anything to destroy Alexander.

—What do you think is going to happen?

The Arcane's eyes turned transparent and he said:

—You can't know.

Both were silent for a while, and then Pyros asked:

—Can I assume my special request has been granted?

—Yes, Timo can leave with you.

—Thank you —said Pyros.

—I will see you soon —said the Arcane, with a hint of a smile. At the door he turned around and said—: You have been a great Guide of Time, Pyros.

—Thank you —replied Pyros, his eyes shining.

A few seconds after the Arcane left, Timo hurried in.

He looked at his master; it was painful to see him so frail.

—Did you hear what he said? —asked Pyros.

Timo nodded.

—Are you ready? —probed Pyros looking at him in the eyes. He already knew the answer.

For Timo there was no reason to live without his master. To be at his side had been his only aspiration in life. He had learned so much, done so much; now it was time to go.

The next morning, they were spirited away to the place where the ceremony was to be held, on a barren beach by the Baltic Sea. In local legend, since the beginning of time sages had come out of the numerous caves in the region to perform strange ceremonies by the seashore. When Pyros, Timo and the other Guides arrived, the villagers looked at them in awe, keeping their distance in respectful silence.

Timo prepared his master for the farewell ritual. He had practised a thousand times what he would do and yet, in that moment, he felt his hands moving clumsily, as if they were tied with knots. He undressed Pyros carefully; he bathed him and dressed him in a white embroidered robe, with a necklace made of lapis-lazuli. All the time he was reciting in his mind the story of his master, as he himself had written it for that moment. Pyros had always taught him to control his emotions, but now that the end was near, Timo could no longer hold back the tears.

For Pyros, the only pain he was carrying on his final journey was Sebastian's treason. Zardoff had been a great disappointment, but what really hurt him was Sebastian's betrayal. Since Pyros first met him, a young and shy monk thirsting for knowledge, Sebastian had had a special place in his heart. He watched him becoming a brilliant scholar, capable of dominating several disciplines, mastering every new thing he learned. Pyros had never known such a passionate student. Timo knew that Pyros would leave on his final journey with that pain and he, faithful as ever, felt it too.

The ceremony was modest. The small procession of thirty men and women, led by Alexander, left the caves at ten at night and congregated on the beach. They recited verses in Pyros's praise, then their voices united in a peaceful and harmonious song in the language of the Guides. That night, shooting stars filled the sky for hours. In the water dolphins kept jumping close to the beach and they were joined by a group of whales making sounds so haunting and powerful that they could be heard many miles away.

It was almost dawn when they saw a sailing boat approaching, with the Arcane standing erect at the bow. Behind him were two giants, the Carriers, who by tradition took the Guides to their final destination. Timo and Alexander lifted Pyros onto the boat; he was asleep now and would never wake up. A breeze started to pick up and with it a suggestion of music, like the sound of pipes. On the boat, Timo sat by Pyros's side while the two Carriers prepared the boat to return to sea. Timo scanned the shore one final time, hoping that Sebastian might still come to say farewell to his master, but he never did.

It was almost dawn when they left. The aurora rewarded them with a calm sea and the first warmth of the morning sun. Timo took one last look around him. After so many centuries, his life was about to end, but he didn't feel sad or anxious. He had had a full life. He could go in peace to his new dwelling. The boat entered a thick mist and Timo felt very sleepy. He lay down by his dear master's side and closed his eyes.

At that precise moment, in a ruined room in the middle of a forest in Belorussia, a fresh breeze played across Sebastian's burning face.

Chapter 14

London, 21st century

—Today is a big day, Ariane —said Mrs Bowman, smiling as I came into the kitchen. With a flourish, she put on the table a plate of scrambled eggs, sausages, bacon, toast and a steaming cup of tea.

—Oh, Mrs Bowman, this is too much for me —I stammered—, I am not used to eating so much in the morning.

—I'm not surprised, you skinny little thing. But it will do you a lot of good. Eat what you can and Pepe will take care of the leftovers.

To my surprise, once I started eating, it was so delicious that I finished everything, and for the first time in my life I knew what it was to feel full. I said goodbye to Mrs Bowman and set off for the Academy. My great adventure was starting!

Out in the street, London and its people were painted in grey colours, but there was something magical about it. I reached the Academy, my heart pounding, and walked tentatively through the imposing columns, almost apologising to the marble floor for stepping on it. A moment later, I was thrilled to see a crowd of young people talking, laughing and greeting each other.

Following Carol's directions, I went to the classroom where my name was listed: Ariane Claret. Until then, I had never felt part of anything; my name had never been included on any list. Almost trembling with fear and excitement, I opened the door and went in. The room smelled like a pleasant mix of wood, paper and dust; the smell of a place that gets old with dignity.

I sat down in the back row, close to the door, and waited. A few minutes later, a girl of roughly my age came in.

—What are you doing here? This is my seat! —she said with a smile that showed her perfect teeth.

—I'm so sorry —I replied, embarrassed.

—I am joking! That's not my seat —she said, giggling—. You look so scared that I couldn't resist teasing. My name is Anita Caracci. What's yours?

—Ariane Claret —I said.

—Pretty name, are you French? I am Italian, Neapolitan to be more precise. The truth is that I wanted to stay in Naples. I miss the weather and the food. But my parents think I need some English phlegm in my blood so, they sent me here to finish my studies. Where are your parents from?

—I...

—Let me see: with those green eyes and that red curly hair, you could be Irish or maybe Scottish.

—Well, I ...

—No, I'm sure you are Irish. Yes, that must be the case. I had a friend who came from Dublin who looked like you even though she was rounder. I bet you don't eat too much. Do people tell you that? My family torments me about food: I am too skinny, they say. I look like an aunt who died when she started to lose weight. Well, of course she died, she weighed ninety kilos, and by the time she decided to lose weight it was already too late! But you didn't answer my question: where are you from?

—I am from Malta —I managed to mumble—, I think... I grew up in an orphanage.

—Ah...—she said, briefly silenced—. I'm sorry, my mother tells me I have a big mouth and she is right. Tell me about you.

I quickly described my life to her, and Anita listened carefully.

—You don't have any family, and I have too much: I have three brothers, seven aunts and uncles and twenty-two cousins. I can share them with you. During our first holidays in two months' time, you will come with me to Naples.

That was how I met Hurricane Nita, as she was called at the Academy.

During the first morning break, she introduced me to her friends —more or less the whole Academy, I found out later. Amidst the turmoil of handshakes, smiles and incomprehensible names, I saw Carol.

—I see you have made some new friends.

—Yes, Anita introduced them to me.

—She is the most popular student, and she will not leave you alone. Actually —she whispered in my ear—, you will be happy to be left alone occasionally.

She was right. I spent the first week in the Academy under Anita's wing, and by the end my head was spinning. She introduced me to all the professors and lots of the students, and insisted I had lunch with her and her group every day. She waltzed through the corridors of the old building as though she had been born there. With her gypsy eyes, her open laugh and her curves, nobody could resist her.

On Saturday, she picked me up from Mrs Bowman's home to take me shopping. She didn't want to see me shivering any more, she said, so she took me to the places where for a few pounds I could get sweaters, shirts and scarves. Then we went to bars where young people without money like me could get together and have a good time.

My first few weeks passed in a whirl of lessons, practices and fun. Besides feeding me with the richest food, Mrs Bowman took me to the wonderful museums spread all over London. We started with the British Museum. I couldn't believe that some of the objects were more than two thousand years old, and I spent hours admiring the remains of fascinating civilisations I had never heard of before.

One day Anita told me mysteriously:

—Mrs Bowman's husband was in the Secret Service.

—How do you know? —I asked, laughing at Anita's expression.

—My father told me. He once met Mr Bowman at a party at the British Embassy in Rome. They all knew he was a spy.

I started to realise that could easily be true. Mrs Bowman had some strange habits. Her front door had three locks on it, in an area of London where people hardly bothered to lock their cars. She didn't answer the phone unless it rang with certain pre-established codes (her daughter's was one ring first, then another call with two rings, and finally the third one with three rings).

She was also obsessed about domestic accidents. Whenever she went out, she would unplug every electrical appliance, and there was a fire extinguisher in every room. Once every three months, she insisted we had an evacuation drill, just in case there was a real emergency. Stop-watch in hand, Mrs. Bowman would measure how long it took us to get to the meeting point in the carpark of an Indian restaurant nearby. On those evenings we had curry at the restaurant, discussing how we could reduce our evacuation time.

—But what do you think might happen? —I asked her the first time we had the drill.

—Anything, Ariane. Here in London there are all sorts of dangers: terrorist attacks, riots, earthquakes, gangs, flooding, not to mention fires which happen every day. But don't worry, we are well prepared and nothing bad will happen to us —she said with the confident smile of an expert.

For Mrs Bowman, part of being well prepared was to fill her basement with tins of food, bottled water, matches, candles, torches and a two-way radio with batteries. Years later, I would find out that Mrs Bowman even had a gun hidden in her basement. The only time she ever used it was to protect me.

Chapter 15

Baghdad, 13th century AD

A pale sun on the yellowish horizon: the beginning of the day in Baghdad, and the only sound was the muezzin's reverential call to prayer.

Abdul al-Naren was about to point his small rug towards Mecca when he heard several knocks on the door. Strange: in all his years working in the Baghdad Library, no visitor had ever shown up so early. He always got to the library very early to clean and tidy the place before the scholars and scientists arrived. Abdul opened the heavy door and saw Tarek al-Kalani, the master's assistant, standing there, looking very agitated.

—In the name of Allah, let me in —his voice was cracking.

—Why so early? I was about to start my prayers...

—We don't have time, we don't have time —said Tarek, closing the door quietly behind him—. We have to leave Baghdad now.

—What's happening? Why do we have to leave?

—You don't understand, Abdul, it's over. Haven't you heard that the Mongols are at Baghdad's gates? There is no way to stop them and soon there will be nothing left, not even the Library.

The word Mongols was itself enough to start Abdul shaking. He had often heard the stories of how they treated their enemies; their cruelty seemed to have no limits. Wherever they went, they left destruction and death.

Tarek continued:

—The master has given us precise instructions: fetch your family, pack your most precious belongings and come back to the Library. We will all meet here.

—But...

—Abdul, this is not the moment to hesitate. You and your family are in serious danger.

Abdul had a deep respect for his master and would never dare to disobey him. But he had never abandoned the Library during the day. It was his duty to be there, receive visitors and translate the texts that the master wanted. He paused for a few seconds and then decided to do as Tarek told him.

He had first come across the Library as a small boy in the streets of Baghdad. His parents had sold him as a slave to a tax collector, who forced him to work long hours in his horse stable, eating scraps and sleeping in the loft. The man soon started to hit Abdul, unmoved by his cries. One day, after a terrible beating, Abdul ran away.

He wandered through the dusty streets, eating what he could steal in the markets and sleeping wherever seemed safe. One morning, he saw a goose waddling down the street. Abdul followed the bird, hoping to catch it, but the goose moved quickly through the narrow streets of the city as if it knew where it was going.

The goose stopped in front of a building of shiny white stone. Abdul had never been there before, but was immediately impressed. It was the tallest building in the city; its doors were made of wood, engraved with rich designs and inscriptions that the boy couldn't understand. The goose turned around and looked at him; then it ran towards a side wall and disappeared through a hole. Abdul followed it.

He had to drag himself through the dirt, bruising his arms and legs, but eventually he reached the other side. He found himself in an exquisite garden, full of flowers and with a fountain in the middle, but he couldn't see the goose anywhere. Instead, a man came out of the building smiling at him. Abdul wanted to run away, but the man stopped him:

—Don't be afraid. I am not going to hurt you.

His voice reassured Abdul. The man had dark eyes, dark hair and a kind expression. He was dressed in a white tunic with a golden cord around his waist.

—First, I will give you something to eat.

Abdul was still scared, but he hadn't eaten since the previous morning, and the mere thought of food made him forget his fears. He followed the man into a kitchen, and the boy thought he was dreaming: on a large table there were plates of fresh fruit, dates, bread, meat and honey.

—Eat as much as you want —said the man smiling, but Abdul wasn't listening. He was already cramming his mouth with the food. When he couldn't eat any more, he couldn't stop himself falling asleep on the floor. Some hours later, he was woken up.

—Now it's time for a good bath —said the man, showing him into a room with a bath full of steaming water.

Abdul had never had a bath before and he was embarrassed to undress in front of a stranger. Reluctantly, he got into the tub with his clothes on. Then the man left the room, telling him to stay as long as he liked, and soon Abdul got distracted with some wooden toys floating in the water.

He started to enjoy the feel of the hot water on his skin, and he lay back in the bath not believing his good luck. Surely, the stranger wanted something from him, but what could he offer? Maybe he wanted him to be his slave. With a master like this, his life would be much better than wandering on the streets. He finished his bath, put on a clean tunic and sandals that the man had left for him, and went out.

The stranger was waiting for him outside:

—Now you look much better —the man said with a smile—. Come, let's talk. Do you know where you are?

Abdul shook his head.

—We are in the Baghdad Library —he said—. It is also called the House of Wisdom, and I am the Rector. Great scientists come here from all over the world to study and teach.

He told the boy the story of the place. The House of Wisdom was founded in the 9th century by the Caliph Harun al–Rashid, as a centre of excellence for Islamic studies. It became even more than that: leading scholars from Persia, India and Greece went there to teach mathematics, astronomy, medicine, alchemy and philosophy. Wise men who were persecuted in the Byzantine Empire or by the ever more intransigent Christian Church were welcomed inside its walls.

Since its foundation, the Baghdad Library had contributed more to science than any other institution, including similar centres in Asia and Europe. It wasn't the first library in the Islamic Empire, but it was the biggest and best known, and it had flourished thanks to the generous donations of caliphs, merchants and army officers. In a society that considered knowledge the greatest wealth, being a benefactor to the Library was a real honour.

—Would you like to stay here? —asked the Rector.

Abdul nodded, and even dared to smile.

—That's what I thought. Come now, it's time to eat again. You haven't told me your name.

—Abdul —he replied and, happy at the thought of more food, followed the Rector into his new life.

As Abdul grew older, he found he had a remarkable talent for learning languages. The Master put him in charge of translating into Arabic many texts written in Greek, Hindu and Latin. When Abdul wasn't busy with his duties, he listened to the scholars who taught in the library, especially his master. Abdul admired his capacity to debate on different topics with as much ease as the specialists in the subject.

One day the Rector said:

—Today I will show you a part of the library that only a few people know about, and one day it may save your life.

They took some narrow stairs down to a basement. At the bottom was a lake that, at first sight, seemed very deep: but when they crossed it, the water came up only to their ankles. When they walked to the other side, Abdul saw five small doors. The Rector chose one and opened it into a tunnel. Holding an oil lamp above his head, the master led Abdul into the darkness of the corridors. They had obviously been excavated for a purpose. As they walked on, they found provisions stored in neat piles, and oil lamps that the Rector lit to continue their journey. Every few hours they stopped to rest, and soon Abdul had lost all sense of time. After what seemed to him like several days underground, eventually they saw a light.

—We are at the end of our journey —said the Rector—. This tunnel ends in the sacred city of Karbala. There are other branches that take you to other cities further away; over time you will know them all. Now it's time for us to return to Baghdad.

The master later told Abdul that it had taken them more than a month to complete their journey. Throughout those long days, the Rector barely ate or slept. He was always busy taking rock samples, trying new corridors, explaining to Abdul how to find his way through the tunnels. That trip left Abdul in no doubt: his master was an exceptional being.

Abdul resumed his life as a translator and Special Guard of the Library. Every few years, he would go back to the tunnels until he became familiar with its twists and bends and could make the journey on his own. Abdul got married and had children, but his loyalty to his master was absolute. His life, he felt, was perfect, which was why the news that Tarek brought him that morning was so devastating.

From the narrow streets outside, he could hear screams and desperate cries. Panic was spreading throughout the city. When Abdul asked a man what was happening, he was told that the soldiers the Caliph had sent to defend the city had all been killed, and the Mongols had already destroyed the city walls. Anyone who tried to escape was being massacred, including women and children. Everywhere, people were gathering their families, looting food stalls, taking whatever they could.

When Abdul finally managed to get home, he found his wife and children cowering in a corner crying with fear. He told them they had to leave, took as much food as he could from the cupboard and then, just as they were about to leave the house, the master arrived.

—You have to go immediately to the Library —he said firmly—. Don't talk to anybody, don't stop, and once you are back in the Library lock the door and don't open it for any reason. I will be there soon and will take you somewhere safe outside the city. Do you remember when I told you that the tunnel might one day save your life? That day has arrived.

—Yes, master, I understand —replied Abdul.— Are we lost?

—The city is lost, Abdul, but we aren't —answered Alexander with a sad smile (2).

(2)"The cost of the Mongol conquest was a civilizational loss of incalculable dimensions. The destruction of libraries, bookshops, observatories, endowed institutions, archives, schools and scriptoria where copyists published the latest works in all fields was devastating...This sharp tear in the civilizational fabric of Central Asia is the most tragic legacy of the Mongol incursion". S. Frederick Starr, 2013. Lost Enlightenment. Princeton Press, pp 466.

Chapter 16

London, 21st century

My first few months at the Academy passed very quickly. After adapting to the long hours of practice, I felt as if I belonged to London and the Academy. I called Sister Ines every week and she was happy just to hear I was happy. The end of the term was getting close, and Anita, as she had promised, invited me to stay at her home in Naples.

Her parents insisted on buying the air ticket for me, and I would offend them if I didn't accept. Or so Anita told me, anyway. When we arrived at Capodichino airport, they were waiting for us. Unlike my friend, her parents were nice without being effusive. Anita introduced me.

—Ariane, we meet you at last —said Anita's mother, Donna Giulia, offering me her hand—. Anita has talked such a lot about you.

—Thank you so much for your generosity —I replied—. Anita has been so kind to me.

—Not at all, Ariane —interrupted the father, Don Mario—. Anita cares about you and she admires you. For us it's a pleasure to have you here.

After a terrifying drive through the streets of Naples, we arrived at the Caraccis' home. They lived in an old building in Posillipo, a few metres from the beach. I could see the wide curve of the Naples Bay, with Vesuvius in the background and the islands of Capri and Ischia beautifully painted on the horizon. My room, with its high ceilings, purple velvet curtains and huge bed with a canopy, was luxury I had never known before. A large window looked out over the Bay and the breeze brought with it a strong smell of the sea. I was stunned by the beauty and the splendour.

I didn't have much time to admire the view, though. Donna Giulia had organised a welcome lunch and the guests were waiting for us downstairs. The dining room had known better times, but it was full of wonderful pieces, like the chandelier made of Capodimonte China, which Anita told me was famous throughout the world. The walls were hung with paintings of Don Mario's ancestors and the floor was covered with a delicate Persian carpet that he told me belonged to Napoleon Bonaparte.

Don Mario was from an aristocratic Neapolitan family linked to the Bourbons. They had once reigned in the south of Italy, and most of their fortune had been squandered by Don Mario's ancestors. All that remained was this mansion. Anita's family lived comfortably, though, thanks to Don Mario's work as an art dealer and Donna Giulia's salary as a professor at the university.

Anita's brothers were already in the dining room, and like their parents, they were not as bubbly as Anita herself. I began to wonder whether she was really as she appeared. Lunch was delicious: home-made pasta, lamb cooked in herbs from the garden, home-grown roasted vegetables and then a Neapolitan Baba, a spongy pudding soaked in enough alcohol to make me dizzy. Don Mario was generous with the wine too. Anita's high spirits helped everyone to relax and I was soon enjoying their funny stories about Neapolitan idiosyncrasies. I learned that San Gennaro, the patron saint of the city, produced a miracle twice a year: his blood —kept in a small bottle in the cathedral— liquefied. If it didn't happen, it was a bad omen for the city. If it took a little longer than expected, the old ladies who spent the day praying to the saint to produce the miracle, would start abusing him with the most vulgar expression of the Neapolitan dialect until he liquefied the blood. Don Mario also told me of the peculiar Neapolitan habit of "adopting" a skull. In the centre of Naples, during excavations work, the contractors discovered several unmarked tombs. The neighbours, feeling sorry for the unknown dead, decided to adopt them, moved them to a nearby church and gave them names, cleaned them and even dressed them. I was starting to see how Neapolitan culture was not only enriched by numerous influences, but it was also deeply rooted in the idea of death.

After lunch, Anita took me on a tour of Naples. She told me its history, starting more than five thousand years ago with the first inhabitants who lived in caves. Later came the Greeks, the Romans, the Normans and the Spanish, until eventually Naples was reunited with the rest of Italy. It had known periods of glory, when it was the biggest port in Europe and one of the world's richest cities; but it had also been cursed by earthquakes and terrible epidemics. Today, it was a city plagued with corruption and traffic. Even so, I found Naples fascinating.

And beautiful too: Anita pointed out the spectacular fortress of Maschio Angioino and the San Carlo theatre, the oldest in Europe. Beneath the city was a labyrinth of catacombs, where the first Neapolitans had buried their dead.

I loved all the history, and even more so a few days later when we went to Pompeii with Don Mario. Until it was destroyed by the eruption of Vesuvius in 79 AD, it had been one of the most prosperous and refined cities in the world. Don Mario described the grandeur and pragmatism of its Roman administration, its vibrant commerce and sophisticated artists, and he entertained us with stories of its uninhibited social life. It was as if the volcano, envious of so much vitality, had decided to show its destructive power.

That same day we also visited the church of the Virgin of the Rosary of Pompeii. Donna Giulia was a fervent Catholic and very interested in my life at the convent. When she asked if I had found a good church in London, I didn't give her an honest answer. I didn't want to tell her that, since I had left Malta, I hadn't been anywhere near a church.

Outside the church was a gypsy woman who offered to read our palms. Donna Giulia gave her some coins but the woman refused them.

—I don't want the money —she said looking at me with a strange look—, I want to read the palm of the girl with red hair.

Anita smiled at me and said:

—Why not, Ariane? It will be fun.

Without waiting for my answer, the gypsy woman took my hand. Then she looked at me with her eyes wide open.

—You are one of them! —she exclaimed.

I thought she was referring to the Caraccis.

—I am a friend of the family.

—I don't mean that —said the woman closing my hand tightly into hers. Her fingers looked like claws and I felt uncomfortable. —You have to be very careful, my dear. They are following you.

—What nonsense —said Anita quickly—, you are scaring my friend. Let's go, Ariane.

The gypsy let me go but kept looking at me as we hurried away. On the way home, Anita told me that the gypsies had become a real nuisance in Naples and were clever pickpockets. When I pointed out that she had actually refused the money, Anita shrugged her shoulders. All rules have their exceptions, she said, even the gypsies of Naples.

***

All too soon, the happiness of my week in Naples came to an end. I had realised how much Anita's friendship meant to me, but also how little I really knew her. She was the first person I could call a friend, but like Naples itself, she had many layers to be discovered.

Soon Christmas was looming up, and both Mrs Bowman and Anita invited me to join their family gatherings. I really wanted to visit Sister Ines, but she herself said I should stay in England. I decided to go with Mrs Bowman to her daughter's house in the Cotswolds, a region famous for its farmed hills and golden-brown buildings.

On Christmas Eve, Mrs Bowman and I took the early train from Paddington. We managed to find a compartment that wasn't full of people, and during the journey, she told me more about her life. Little did I imagine that during that Christmas holiday, I would have a scary and extraordinary experience.

Chapter 17

Strasbourg, 15th century

—The numbers don't add up, sir —said the accountant, mortified— we can't continue with the project.

—I know, Victor —said Gutenberg, obviously worried—. But isn't there some way to convince the investors to wait a year, until things get back to normal in Aachen?

—The problem is that they don't believe the exhibition will happen, not even when the city recovers. They are asking for their money back.

It was not the first time Victor had seen Gutenberg in this predicament, with an extraordinary idea but hamstrung by debts. At various stages, Johannes Gutenberg had been ironmonger, jeweller and printer, but he had never been successful. On this occasion, though, it wasn't his fault.

When Gutenberg had moved to Strasbourg, thanks to his aristocratic standing and his cultivated manners, he was welcomed into its social circles. It didn't take him long to find backers for his ideas. But money doesn't follow failure, and Gutenberg was too chaotic and unstable for the rich men of Strasbourg. Soon they were demanding stringent safeguards for their money.

The Aachen project seemed a safe one. To commemorate Emperor Charlemagne, the municipal authorities had asked Gutenberg to produce mirrors of polished metal which, as was the belief at the time, could absorb divine light from religious relics. Some investors got excited by the project and put up a lot of money for Gutenberg to produce the mirrors, which the city council guaranteed to buy.

Once again, luck was not on Gutenberg's side. Aachen was battered by heavy rain and flooding, and the local authorities had to divert all the money they had promised for the mirrors. Gutenberg had already bought the materials, paid money on account to the craftsmen and for transport, but without the municipal funds he didn't have the money to complete the project or to store the raw materials. Worse, he would soon have to tell the investors that he couldn't return their money. His position was desperate, and he knew it. His only consolation was to continue with his secret project, the one that really fascinated him.

When the young Gutenberg had learned how to read, his father had given him a book about Roman history. In that moment, his life had changed. He touched the pages with reverence, tracing with his fingers the beautiful hand-written letters, trying to imagine the man who had devoted so many hours to writing down the story of the Roman Empire. His passion for books grew and, after working every morning in his father's workshop as a blacksmith, he would go to his room to read until late at night.

His family belonged to the rich merchant class in Mainz, but they lost everything during civil unrest and rioters burnt their house. The Gutenbergs and many other families were forced to leave Mainz. The only thing the young Johannes took with him was a copy of Homer's Iliad. The experience changed his life again. He kept asking himself what was the reason for inequality, which had caused so much resentment and social violence. There was only one answer: ignorance.

In Gutenberg's time, printing a book was an expensive and laborious process. To carve from a piece of wood each letter of a text, to make sure the letters were aligned, to clean the borders to make sure the ink didn't spill —all this could take months. Worse, wood wore out very quickly, so producing more copies involved the same process all over again. Books for the masses were simply unavailable, which meant that mass education was impossible. Gutenberg wanted to find a way to make knowledge accessible for everybody, rich and poor, and that was his secret project.

He rented an old farm house outside Strasbourg, where he installed some experimental equipment. During the day he worked on his official projects. At night he spent hours at the farm house, surviving on very little sleep.

That day, after the depressing conversation with the accountant, Gutenberg went to the farm house. There, all his worries disappeared and he could dream. He lit a candle, laid a fire with dry logs, opened a cupboard and took out a bottle of wine, a piece of bread and some cheese, and sat down to eat.

On the table where he worked were some copper prototypes he was testing. Gutenberg was convinced that metal letters wouldn't wear out as wood did, and thanks to his experience as a blacksmith, it was easy for him to produce the alphabet and the typographic symbols in copper. Being a perfectionist, for his tests Gutenberg only used paper and ink that he himself had produced. He knew they were the right material for his metal prototypes.

He was finishing his glass of wine when he heard a knock at the door. It startled him; nobody knew about the farm house, and for a second he thought it must be a debt-collector. Gutenberg looked cautiously through the window and was surprised to see a well-dressed man smiling at him through the glass. He wasn't sure whether to open the door, but his curiosity was stronger than his prudence.

—I apologise for knocking at your door so late at night —said the stranger—. I saw a light and I thought you must still be awake. Let me introduce myself: my name is Alexander Von Rossen and I am travelling east. My horse is tired, I have been on the road for many days, and yours is the only light I have seen for many miles.

—It is not safe to travel at night —said Gutenberg, still feeling uncomfortable.

—That's what I have been told, Sir, but in this case it was worth taking a risk. It is a pleasure to meet the great Gutenberg.

—How do you know my name?

—If you let me in, I will tell you. It is after eleven and it is cold outside. I just need to warm up and let my horse rest. I will leave very early in the morning.

Cautiously checking that nobody else was hiding outside, Gutenberg let the stranger in.

—Thank you very much —said Alexander, taking his cloak off.

—You still haven't told me how you know my name —insisted Gutenberg.

—Maybe you will be surprised to hear that amongst my people you are considered a genius. I recognised your face immediately.

—How could you recognise me? Nobody has done my portrait. Who are your people . Where do you come from?

Gutenberg looked at him suspiciously. The stranger's clothes and manners marked him out as a gentleman, but the fact that he had arrived at that time of the night and knew Gutenberg's name made him think that he was a debt-collector, or, even worse, someone who would try to copy his ideas. That had happened several times in the past. Reluctantly, but unwilling to stifle his curiosity, Gutenberg invited his visitor to sit down, and offered him some wine.

—I come from the lands in the north —said Alexander—, beyond the Urals, where scientists and philosophers are more respected than rulers and warriors.

—It must be a very civilised place —said Gutenberg sarcastically—. I didn't know that a country like that existed. Nowadays only money and power matter. Respect for knowledge disappeared with the ancient civilisations.

—Our people are not well known, we prefer to live isolated from the rest of the world, but we love philosophy and science, and whenever possible we have to learn from other people, like you. To you, Gutenberg —said Alexander, raising his goblet. He continued—: Our ambition is the same as yours: we want to educate the masses, especially the poorest. We know you have been trying different ways of producing books. I was very lucky to find you.

Gutenberg stared at the stranger trying to work out his real intentions. How did he know about his experiments? Yes, most likely he was a spy. By now Gutenberg's suspicions were struggling against tiredness; he had had a long day. Little by little, while the stranger was talking, he felt his eyelids closing, thought he could hear soft music and drifted into a deep sleep.

It was almost six in the morning when Johannes woke up. He looked around for his visitor, but the room was empty. For a moment, Gutenberg panicked: maybe the man had stolen something. Quickly, he checked his cluttered desk; nothing was missing, but anyway, his idea might have been copied. He had to continue his work immediately.

The cold of the night had numbed his body; he threw more wood on the fire and boiled some water. He looked at the window: the sky was pale blue and the sun was just coming over the horizon when, all of a sudden, a ray of light struck him and a loud noise shook the house. Gutenberg fell to the floor. Next, half-conscious, he got to his feet, feeling as if he were floating.

In front of him, there was a wine press; on one side it had several letters bunched together and glistening with ink. A sheet of paper fell softly onto the letters, and the other side of the press slowly descended. Then, just as slowly, it rose again, and on the sheet Gutenberg saw two beautifully printed words.

In principio

The copper letters moved, rearranging themselves, and again the press descended onto the paper. This time he read:

creavit Deus

Gutenberg understood. He ran outside to the barn, where he had once stored an old grape press, and found it under piles of straw. He dragged it into the house and spent the rest of the day and night working. By then he had set up a metal frame on which the letters could slide. He chose some from the ones he had been using in his previous tests. He brushed them with ink, put the paper on the press and then he lowered the other side and gradually lifted it. On the paper, in bright red, firm and clear, were printed the first lines of Genesis:

In principio creavit Deus caelum et terram.

Terra autem erat inanis et vacua,

Et tenebrae super faciem abyssi,

Et spiritus Dei ferebatur super aquas

Gutenberg rushed to change the letters, repeated the procedure, and the next words were just as familiar, just as perfect:

Dixitque Deus: "Fiat lux". Et facta est lux.

Et vidit Deus lucem quod esset bona

Et divisit Deus lucem ac tenebras

Gutenberg had invented a way to print books in large numbers, accessible to the masses. That one night in the 15th century opened the door to the wonders of knowledge, transforming human destiny from then on.

Chapter 18

Cotswolds, 21st century

During the train journey to Oxfordshire, Mrs Bowman talked about her husband. She had had a very exciting life by his side —in every sense, she remarked with a wink. Behind his formal role as cultural attaché, he had actually been a spy. Mr Bowman rose to become the head of Britain's counter-Soviet espionage during the Cold War. He had sometimes been away from home for weeks, and all she knew was that her husband was on a special mission. Although she never knew the details, she talked about him with such admiration, as if he had single-handedly been responsible for the fall of the Berlin Wall.

My landlady's revelations entertained me throughout the journey, until we arrived at a small village called Kingham, where Emily and Harry were waiting for us with a very excited Helena. The young couple had converted an old barn into a two-storey house, surrounded by a tidy garden that had some colour even at that time of the year. Inside, the house had high ceilings, an open-plan kitchen and a dining area with a big chimney. Upstairs the rooms were cosy and each also had a chimney. Helena insisted on showing me her room, with light wall paper and illustrations from "Alice in Wonderland". The house's atmosphere contrasted with the grey sky and the barren fields, but the weather didn't dampen our spirits, especially when Emily announced she was pregnant.

I helped the family decorate the house and put up a tall pine tree in a corner of the sitting room. Helena's excitement was infectious, and I couldn't help thinking of all the sad and dull Christmases I had spent in the orphanage. Still, I realised how much I missed Sister Ines, and I wished she were here with me.

On Christmas Eve we went to Church for midnight mass. It was the first time I had attended an Anglican Mass, and it left me perplexed. The priest was a smiley and kind woman who, rather than performing a solemn ritual, spent a lot of time chatting to the worshippers. When the time came for the congregation to receive the bread and wine, Mrs Bowman stood up and asked me, surprised:

—Aren't you coming?

—I am Catholic, it would be heresy —I whispered.

She, shrugging her shoulders, replied:

—Not here it isn't. Come with me.

I hesitated but then, just to please her, I walked up to the altar. As usual, the Communion didn't move me, but this time I didn't feel guilty.

I woke up early on Christmas day and decided to walk around the fields close to the house. It had snowed a bit during the night and the soft hills of the Cotswolds were sprinkled with white; there was something magical in the air. Sheathed in a warm coat and thick snow boots, I left the house. There was an hour before breakfast, and I decided to go to an old mill I had noticed the day before. The snow crunched under my feet, and the wind was soon making me shiver, but the crystal-clear blue sky and the pure air were enchanting.

After walking for ten minutes across the fields, I saw a man coming in my direction. In the emptiness of the country-side and so early on Christmas day, it seemed strange to cross paths with somebody else. As we got closer, I could see he was tall and olive-skinned. He smiled at me with his green eyes and said:

—Good morning and Happy Christmas. It's quite cold today, isn't it?

He didn't look British, and his accent was unfamiliar.

—Good morning and Happy Christmas to you too —I wanted to keep walking, but he kept talking.

—Do you live around here?

—No, I am staying with friends —I said—, and you?

—I'm a stranger too. I am spending the holidays with my brother and his family.

That was enough conversation for me, but he kept going:

—What do you do?

—I'm studying music.

—How lovely! It must be re...

Before he could go any further, a piercing sound rang out and I felt something brush the back of my coat. The man grabbed my arm and pulled me to the ground.

—That was a bullet!—he exclaimed—. Are you OK?

—Yes, I suppose so —I replied, shocked.

—Be careful! —he shouted towards the copse at the edge of the field—. There are people walking here.

We heard some scuffling from the road and then absolute silence.

—Crazy —the man said, his face worried— what did he think he was doing?

—Th...thanks —I was shaking so much I could barely mumble.

—Don't worry, this kind of things is very rare in England. Anyway, let me take you home.

I couldn't stop shaking as we walked back to the barn, and was greatly relieved to get to the front door.

—I am very sorry you got scared —said the man—, especially on Christmas day. I can only imagine that was a novice who didn't realise the dangers of a loaded gun.

—I don't know how to thank you —I replied, still stunned— you saved my life .

—Don't worry ...by the way, what's your name?

—Ariane.

—That's a musical name —he managed a smile—. My name is Zaher Dawy by the way.

—Do you want to come in for a cup of tea? —I asked.

—No thanks, I have to get back. My brother will be worried. But I will leave you my card, just in case we meet again and you still want to offer me that cup of tea.

Professor Zaher Dawy, from the University of Beirut, said the card and, to my astonishment, in one corner was the familiar image: a blue two-pointed feather with a coloured spot in the middle. I looked at him confused, and he smiled.

—I hope your studies go well and perhaps our paths will cross again —he said, shaking my hand and then turning quickly away.

Quietly I went inside, but Mrs Bowman was up and she noticed I was shaking. When I told her about the rifle shot, she was very upset. That kind of thing didn't happen in the Cotswolds, and anyway shooting with a rifle was tightly controlled. I showed Emily the card the professor had given me, but she didn't know anyone in the village called Dawy.

—Poor Ariane —said Mrs Bowman—. Let me get you some camomile tea.

—Thank you Mrs Bowman, that's just what I need.

She replied firmly:

—This is why we need to keep our eyes open, we aren't safe anywhere!

Little Helena was listening in silence, her face pale. Emily quickly changed the subject, her voice artificially cheerful:

—All well now! Let's get on with Christmas. Ariane, would you like some breakfast?

Chapter 19

Cambridge, 17th century

The afternoon light was fading and some faint stars were starting to spot the sky. A fresh breeze crossed the well-kept gardens of Trinity College, Cambridge, ruffling the last wallflowers that announced the end of autumn. Isaac Newton was looking down from one of the college's windows, indifferent to the change of season, submerged in the peace of his favourite time of the day, his commitments over.

Already considered one of the most remarkable scientists of his time, for Newton there wasn't a bigger pleasure than the solitude of his lab. He never got married, had very few friends, wasn't interested in social life and more than once had public and explosive rows with his colleagues. His isolation was not only because of his disagreements with the academic establishment, but mainly because of his rejection of the Anglican hierarchy which had caused controversy in the University.

***

Isaac Newton was born in 1643, a premature baby, weak and small, in Woolsthorpe, a village in the north of England. As a child he never played with his contemporaries and was no more than mediocre in the classroom. As he grew up, his only interest was in building windmills and water clocks.

After failing as a farmer, the occupation his mother had wished for him, Newton managed to get a place at Trinity College. In 1665, because of the bubonic plague, the university had to close and Isaac went back home for two years until the epidemic passed. During those years, he studied science and philosophy, and between 1665 and 1667 —the period he later called Anni mirabiles— he worked out the solution for binomial power, which laid the foundations for classical mechanics. Newton made seminal contributions to optics, and he shares credit with Gottfried Leibniz for the development of calculus. He built the first reflecting telescope and developed a theory of colour based on the observation that a prism decomposes white light into the many colours of the visible spectrum. He formulated an empirical law of cooling, studied the speed of sound, and introduced the notion of Newtonian fluid. In addition to his work on calculus, as a mathematician Newton contributed to the study of power series, generalised the binomial theorem to non-integer exponents, developed a method for approximating the roots of a function, and classified most of the cubic plane curves. In his notebook he wrote the motto that defined his career:

Amicus Plato,

Amicus Aristoteles

Magis amica veritas

"Plato is my friend. Aristotle is my friend. But my best friend is truth"

After the plague was over, Newton went back to Cambridge in 1668. The university authorities were so impressed by what he had been doing that he was appointed professor emeritus. Newton never considered himself a genius, and he attributed his success to the fact that he spent more time on his studies than others did. Nobody though knew about Newton's obsession with the occult.

He spent entire nights studying ancient texts, including the Bible, from which he concluded that Jesus Christ was born not in December but in April. From that he deduced that the world would end not in 1757, as the Anglican Church said, but in 2060, the result of a comet colliding with the Earth.

Newton had England's largest collection of books on Alchemy, and translated several ancient books on the subject. Although he didn't formally belong to any sect, he had frequent contact with the followers of Socinianism and Arianism, two spiritual movements that rejected the fundamental principles of the Anglican faith. He kept his exchanges with these groups completely secret.

Newton never openly admitted his beliefs, as he didn't want to attract even more controversy. He was already clashing with fellow academics, and his public disputes with Gottfried Leibniz were so fierce that they became the talk of the Academic establishment. He took on the prestigious role of Lucasian Professor at Cambridge University, obtaining government exemption from the usual requirement that the post be held by an ordained Church of

England priest. It was this that prompted the widespread rumour that he was a heretic.

And Newton was a heretic. Although a convinced monotheist, he didn't believe in the Holy Trinity nor in the divine nature of Jesus Christ, whom he saw as merely a mediator between God and mankind. Newton didn't believe that the Saints and the Virgin Mary should be glorified; in his view, men could adore only the unique and true God.

Newton thought that science provided the tools to understand God's principles. The organised dynamism of the universe had been created by a God, and it was the duty of every scientist to discover the true nature of the universe through reason. He was convinced that, many centuries earlier, wise men knew the truth about God; science was only rediscovering what was already known. Alchemy and the Hermetic texts contained the secret codes of the natural order and the future of mankind.

With such radical ideas, it wasn't difficult to understand why Newton preferred to isolate himself from his colleagues and take refuge in his laboratory. There, in a labyrinth of test tubes, burners, gold, lead and other metals, he could search for the alchemist's dream: the Philosopher's Stone, the process that would transform an element into gold.

He was thinking about that when a college servant brought him a letter from the Duke of Olborough. The Duke was the most prominent aristocrat in Cambridge and a great benefactor of the university. Inside the envelope was an invitation to a speech about the latest archaeological excavations in Egypt and the possible discovery of the original Emerald tablet, the mysterious code of the Hermetic.

It was a topic that enthralled Newton. The oldest transcript known of the Emerald tablet at the time had been written in Arabic and was found in Egypt, but it was not the original text It contained the secrets of the Hermetic sect, the first known sect in ancient history. Even though it was highly unlikely that the original tablet had been found, he immediately sent back his answer with the servant, accepting the invitation. If the speech happened to be a bore, he wouldn't have any problem in standing up and leaving, as he had done many times before. Courtesy was not one of Newton's virtues.

On the night of the conference it was snowing lightly and Newton was wrapping himself in his coat when somebody knocked at the door. It was Halley, England's most renowned astronomer and one of Newton's few friends.

—I thought you would be going to the speech as well. Let's walk together, I have several things to discuss with you.

While walking across the court of Trinity, Halley sounded excited:

—Have you had a chance to review the estimates that Hooke and I have made about the force of attraction between planets?

—Hooke, that annoying man! —said Newton—. Meddling in all sorts of things without getting anywhere. And then, when somebody gets any result in any of the subjects Hooke has superficially touched, he accuses them of plagiarism. I can't stand him!

Newton had had several disagreements with Hooke in the recently established Royal Society. Halley continued talking, as if he hadn't heard Newton's outburst.

—Based on our estimates, the planets' orbits are elliptical, but we don't understand why.

Newton didn't say a word, but he was genuinely surprised. He had been asking himself the same question, and he had a hypothesis; but the empirical evidence didn't corroborate it and he still couldn't establish a satisfactory theory.

At the Duke's manor, a butler received the guests and directed them to the library. The house was as extravagant as its owner, filled with gigantic turtle shells, dinosaur skeletons, massive rocks and precious paintings. When Newton entered the library, people fell silent; it was very unusual to see him at a social event, particularly at night.

—Do you see that table? —said Halley, admiring the furniture—. Apparently it belonged to Copernicus when he was studying medicine in Padua. Anyway, that's what the Duke says.

But Newton was more interested in the artefacts on the table: papyrus, sculptures in stone and clay representing Hermetic symbols, and a rectangular wooden box adorned with a delicate carving of a feather with two points. A few minutes later the Duke came in with the speaker, a man with a pleasant smile, elegantly dressed and with unusually dark eyes. The Duke was wearing his dressing gown and slippers and —living up to his eccentric image— he had a monkey on his shoulder. He introduced his guest as Baron Alexander Von Rossen, one of the most experienced archaeologists on the continent. He then left the room, undoubtedly to go to sleep.

The speaker started:

—First of all, thank you for coming here this evening. I am honoured to have in the audience so many remarkable scientists. As my kind host said, I am an archaeologist and my main area of interest is Egypt. My team and I have spent almost three decades excavating sites in the Upper Nile and the Western Desert.

Newton started to pay more attention. Von Rossen continued:

—The majority of the tombs and buildings that we excavated had been looted. Only a few interesting artefacts remained, but during our last expedition my team dug out a fort close to a village called El Ashmunein that, perhaps because of its isolation, was intact. We found a necropolis and a temple apparently dedicated to the god Thoth, known by the Greeks as Hermes. The construction style indicates that the fort was built around two thousand years before Christ, which would make it the oldest in the region.

He paused and looked at the audience.

—The pieces you see on the table were in the temple, but the most interesting piece is in this box.

Von Rossen carefully opened the wooden box, and turned it towards the audience so they could see. Several people gasped, and even Newton was stunned.

—As you can see —continued Von Rossen— this is an emerald tablet carved with hieroglyphic script. It is intact, which means that, at the time, it must have been the biggest emerald ever found. Our preliminary researches lead us to believe that this could be the original Emerald Tablet of the Hermetic. The meaning of the hieroglyphs on the stone is similar to what is written in the Arabic version we all know about, which dates back to about 500 AD. This emerald is much older and has much more information about the Hermetic. We suppose that this original tablet was copied and translated later, intentionally excluding some important information.

A murmur rippled around the room. Newton, uninterested in the comments of the audience, recognised the symbols. They were indeed the same as those on the Emerald Tablet he knew so well. They set out a list of rules, a code of conduct for achieving the highest levels of spirituality. But the Baron was right. In the tablet the man held in his hands, there was much more: magical rituals and secret practices reserved only for those initiated into the cult.

—The style of the hieroglyphs is the same as other inscriptions we found in the fort —Von Rossen said—, which makes them around three thousand years old. This discovery will help us to understand better the philosophy of the Hermetic sect.

At that point, Halley stood up and said in a loud voice:

—The greatest expert in this matter is here tonight: Isaac Newton.

The audience looked around Newton, who upset by the unwelcome attention, said:

—I only translated a few of the Hermetic texts. The "Emerald Tablet" was one of them, and it was a long time ago —and all the while he was asking himself: how could Halley know about his Hermetic studies?

—We have read your work carefully, Professor Newton —said Von Rossen—. We used it as a guide for our expedition.

Newton felt even more uncomfortable. Halley might have seen him working on the Hermetic studies on the many occasions he had visited Newton, but how could a perfect stranger have read it? He had never published it! Fortunately, the audience was now busy asking the Baron questions, and he answered each one of them patiently.

At the end of the meeting, several people from the audience approached Von Rossen to continue talking. Newton would have done so as well, but he was tired and in a bad mood. His house was close by and, still upset with Halley, he decided to leave on his own.

Just as he was nearing his own front door, he heard a voice behind him:

—Professor Newton.

He turned around and was surprised to see Von Rossen.

—I hope I am not bothering you. I wanted to talk to you after the conference, but the other guests didn't allow me to —he said with a smile.

—Oh, yes, I also wanted to talk to you —answered Newton.

—Do you mind if I join you?

—Not at all.

—I thought you might like to see the tablet again and even tell me more about your studies on the topic.

Newton, wary again, wondered how Von Rossen knew about his research.

—Unless it's not what you want —said the Baron.

—I would like to know how you found out about my research on Hermetic studies.

—We move in the same circles, Professor —replied Von Rossen—. Like you, we have an open mind and we ask ourselves questions about the truth of the religious consensus. Some of what we say is not accepted by scientists, religious leaders and even governments, which is why we keep our activities quite secret.

Newton glanced at the Baron, suspecting he knew much more about him than he was saying. Von Rossen continued:

—In every society, the established order doesn't tolerate doubt, because it is uncomfortable. Religious leaders are afraid, because it would make them lose control over the worshippers. In the academic world, to have doubts is taken as a sign of intellectual weakness; the greatest scientists are quick to scorn any idea that doesn't have a solid mathematical or factual base. But the world is not only what we can see and touch. Only individuals who are brave enough to live in constant doubt, who have the urge to keep inquiring, can make significant contributions to the progress of mankind. You are one of those, Professor Newton.

Newton understood what Von Rossen's words meant. He reckoned the Baron probably belonged to one of those sects that flourished outside Christianity, the sort that Newton criticised in public but approached privately. Even so, he didn't know enough about him to trust him. Newton changed the subject:

—Do you really think you have found the Hermetic "Emerald Tablet"?

—The content is the same as the Arabic texts, but on this tablet we also found new codes. They clearly refer to the Hermetic philosophy and rituals. In the fort there were other artefacts that were probably used in ceremonies.

—Up to now, I never thought it was a real object: it seemed more like a symbol.

—It is real —the Baron replied.

—Then show it to me —said Newton.

Moving a pile of papers, the Baron carefully put the box on the table and opened it. For the second time that evening, Newton was astonished. Close up, the emerald was even more impressive. He picked up a magnifying glass and scrutinised the hieroglyphs; he touched the stone and felt as if a current was rushing through his body. He couldn't believe what he was looking at.

For a while, the two men discussed the possible origins of the tablet. Then, to Newton's delight, the Baron suggested that he might like to keep it for some time, to decipher the text. Barely trying to conceal his eagerness, Newton said he would do so.

—Good —said Von Rossen—. Now it's time for me to go. You look tired and I have to leave early tomorrow —and he walked to the door.

Newton was too tired to undress, falling asleep with his clothes on. A few hours later, his servant peeped into the room, put out the fire and took Newton's shoes off; but his master was so fast asleep that he didn't stir.

A week later, Newton had to go back to Woolsthorpe, where his siblings still lived; they needed help to sort out their parents' inheritance. He got there in time for lunch, and afterwards he decided to go for a walk. During the past few days, he had been preoccupied with the "Emerald Tablet", but, subconsciously, he kept recalling Halley's question about the planets' orbits. He went into the garden and sat down on a bench, deep in his thoughts. A few steps away was an apple tree, and Newton was surprised to see that although it had only a few leaves left, apples were still hanging from its branches.

He closed his eyes and let his mind wander from one thought to another. When he opened them again, he took another look at the tree and he saw an apple falling slowly, very slowly, to the ground. Suddenly, Newton jumped from the bench. Of course! The answer to Halley's question had been staring him in the face all the time. The same reason the apple fell was also why all celestial bodies are related to each other: any two bodies in the universe attract each other with a force that is directly proportional to the product of their masses and inversely proportional to the square of the distance between them. The same force would explain the shape of the planets' orbits. Getting more and more excited, he made some quick mental calculations and hurried back home. A few weeks later, Isaac Newton established the basis of the theory of universal gravitation.

Newton was called "The last magician"(3). His passion for the occult was even more powerful than his interest in science, but his contributions to calculus, astronomy and optics were extraordinary.

Nature and Nature's Law lay hid in Night:

God said, "Let Newton be!" and all was light

Epithaph on Isaac Newton

by Alexander Pope

(3)vRossi, P. 2006. Il tempo dei maghi. Raffaello Cortina Editore. p.5

Chapter 20

London, 21st century

—This weather is not for humans —said Anita, soaking wet and grumbling—. I don't know why my parents sent me to this country. I can't stand the cold. Why didn't they choose Africa or Australia?

—Then we wouldn't have met —I replied, and Anita grinned. It didn't take much to get her to smile.

Maybe because of her sunny character, Anita didn't fit into the grey and melancholic colours of the British winter. I was fine; I even felt protected by the low clouds, the fine rain and the fog.

Anita was an accomplished violinist, the best in her class. During theory lessons, she used to sit with me in case I needed help. It all changed when an attractive American violinist joined the Academy in the new year and she went back to her group. I really didn't need her any more. I had caught up with the theory and it even became one of my favourite subjects.

I had finished my first year with good grades, and both Christopher and Carol congratulated me when they gave me the Academic Excellence Award. My scholarship depended on my performance, so I had a big incentive to do well, though I didn't need one. I loved studying and practising and I loved my life at the Academy. Every day reminded me of what I had missed growing up in the orphanage, and how lucky I was to escape.

On the last day of the summer term, I was walking to the bus stop from the Academy when I heard somebody calling me. When I turned around, I didn't immediately recognise the young woman smiling at me.

—Have you forgotten me? I am Eliza, from the orphanage. Don't you remember?

—Eliza, of course! I am sorry, I just didn't expect to see you in London. What are you doing here?

—I am in town for a couple of days and I came to see you. I knew you were studying at the Academy.

—What a surprise!

—You look really well, Ariane. Leaving the orphanage was a good thing —she said with a big smile—. Let's have a cup of tea.

Eliza and I walked through Piccadilly and found somewhere we could order tea and scones. She told me she had left Malta because she was bored of living on an island, and now was travelling through Europe. She hadn't changed at all and had the same relaxed and carefree attitude that made her so charming.

I decided to tell her how, when we first met at the orphanage, I wasn't quite sure whether my midnight visitor was real or just a product of my imagination. I felt slightly embarrassed as I told her my story, but she laughed in delight.

—What a thought —she said—. And you know what? Perhaps you were closer to the truth than you realised.

With this remark hanging in the air, I changed the subject.

—What about the pets? —I asked.

—I left them in Malta with a good friend who would take care of them, but I brought you this.

From her bag, she produced a beautiful two-pointed feather with a silver dot on a hair clip.

—What a strange coincidence! —I couldn't get over my surprise.

—What coincidence? —Eliza asked.

—I have seen this feather before.

—Yes, I know. In your diary.

—How do you know it was in my diary?

—You told me.

—No, I didn't. I never told anyone— I was even more perplexed.

—Of course you did. Anyway, let's not argue about it. Do you like it?

—Yes, of course, it's beautiful. Thank you —I said, but I was still baffled. I was sure I had never mentioned the two-pointed feather to Eliza.

She then started talking about her travels, and soon we were happily chatting again. At around five she had to leave.

—I am so happy to see you in such good form, Ariane.

—I am happy to see you too, Eliza.

—Well, I guess this is it. I have to leave tonight and will be travelling for quite some time. But I do hope we will see each other again.

—I hope so too, Eliza. Now that you know how to find me, please let me know when you are back to London.

—I will.

She gave me a hug, and I had a strong feeling I would see her again.

***

During the summer I had been giving private tuition, which meant I could save some money. I found out that in London, I could do a lot with very little. Busy every day, and most evenings too, I soon got out of the habit of writing to Sister Ines and I didn't call her. One day the phone rang. It was Sister Francesca:

—Ariane, what happened, my darling girl, that you haven't called? Poor Sister Ines was taken ill and had to go to the hospital. We thought it was a heart attack, but thank

God and the Holy Virgin Mary, she has a heart stronger than a horse. She had had a nervous breakdown, because she was so worried about you.

—I am very sorry, Sister Francesca! —I replied, feeling like a monster —. I am fine, I have just been very busy.

—Here is Sister Ines, she didn't want to call because she was afraid she would get bad news. Here she is.

—Ariane —Sister Ines's cracked voice broke my heart—. Are you alright? Are they treating you well? You can come back whenever you want, you know that the doors to this house are always open.

—Sister Ines, I'm so, so sorry I haven't called you! I am fine, I promise you. And I also promise you that from now on you will hear from me every week.

And that was what I did until the day Sister Ines died a few months later. She didn't have a horse's heart after all. When Sister Francesca called to give me the news, she told me that when Sister Ines died she was holding her rosary and a picture of me as a little child. To lose Sister Ines was very painful; she had been the closest thing to a true mother I had had, and I realised how much I had learned from her. She had asked the other nuns to send me her few possessions: a prayer book, pictures mostly of me, her good luck rosary and some linen handkerchiefs that she had embroidered for me for my eighteenth birthday. That was the last contact I had with the nuns who had raised me.

Instead, my friendship with Mrs Bowman grew stronger every day. In my second year she decided not to charge me for the room anymore. I only had to contribute to the food, "so that I could have a little bit more pocket money", she said. We often went to the cinema or the theatre together. Mrs Bowman loved musicals, and London was the place to enjoy them. Emily visited her every week and Helena came on Wednesdays, although I only saw her from time to time. I loved that simple domestic routine, and felt I was part of it for the first time in my life.

Occasionally, I needed to be on my own, to read a book or take a long walk. I still couldn't shake off a feeling of nostalgia that, buried in a corner of my mind, sometimes told me something important was missing.

It was during that year that I had my first relationship. Andy Hopps was a timid, awkward English boy with deep blue eyes, who blushed every time he spoke to me. Anita teased me about him, and I am sure she was the one who gave him my phone number.

—It's for you —called Mrs Bowman from the corridor, when I was washing my hair.

I put my head in a towel, came out from the bathroom and noticed her mischievous smile.

—Hello, who is it, please?

—Ariane? It is... Andy, Andy Hopps, from the Academy.

I felt my face burning under Mrs Bowman's scrutiny.

—Oh, yes Andy. What a surprise!

—Yes... well...Would you like to come to a movie on Sunday and then maybe have a pizza? I mean... if you want ...

—Yes, of course. What time?

—I can pick you up at six.

—Perfect, see you on Sunday then.

—So? —Mrs Bowman's smile was almost childishly naughty.

—Nothing, he's just a classmate.

—He has a very nice voice. Does he sing?

—No, he plays the trombone.

—Ah.

She seemed slightly disappointed about the trombone, but on Sunday afternoon she helped me to find the right dress and combed my hair —more out of control than ever— into a tidy bun. Andy arrived punctually at six and we went to the movies. We had a great time, although my hairdo collapsed with the first drops of rain.

With the blessing of Anita and Mrs Bowman, Andy and I developed a juvenile love that fuelled my zest for life. I embraced the belated awakening of my femininity, navigating happily through the next few years until the day I met Will.

***

I graduated from the Academy with top marks. Unusually —I was told the last time it had happened was twenty-five years ago— I had been offered the chance to continue my studies while also performing with the Academy's orchestra. I was eighteen years old and had the world at my feet. I didn't want to leave Mrs Bowman — Elspeth as she asked me to call her— but with my new life came more opportunities to travel. I took them all, as if I wanted to discover everything at once.

One autumn evening I gave a performance at the Wigmore Hall. I played For Elise, the same piece I had been set in Valletta when I was being tested for the Academy two years earlier. Just two years! It seemed like a lifetime, and Beethoven's piano concert proved to be just as much of a life-changer that evening as it was in Valletta.

As I came out of the Wigmore Hall, a young man walked up to me. To my surprise, he handed me a white rose, slightly squashed.

—I tried to throw it onto the stage but I missed, so I collected it again to give to you in person. It was the least I could do.

—Oh, thank you. You shouldn't have bothered.

—I have never heard Beethoven played with such feeling.

I took a second look at the young man in front of me, tousled, tall and lanky, who smiled at me with his bright brown eyes. From that moment on, we were together.

Will was a journalist, his mind quick and bright, and he was enthusiastic about almost everything. He loved classical music, so he came to my performances and rehearsals whenever he could; and when his job allowed, he even came on tour with me. We went together to Brussels, Amsterdam, Prague, Vienna and Milan, and three years after we met, he asked me to marry him. I felt too young for such a commitment, but Will was ten years older than me. He was keen to settle down and have a family.

Neither Elspeth nor Anita liked the idea of my getting married. I was just twenty-two, and when I asked Carol's opinion, she said I would be spending a lot of time on tour both in Britain and the rest of Europe. It would be difficult to have a family life at that stage in my career. Those objections didn't bother Will. He was convinced we were meant to be together, it was inevitable, so why waste time? I didn't resist his arguments, partly because he was himself irresistibly keen, but also because I longed for stability and family life. The scars from the orphanage had not disappeared.

We got married one morning in May in a civil ceremony in the beautiful gardens of Battersea Park, beside the Thames. The sky was crystalline blue and the sun warmed the spring air. His family and our best friends were there, and as a surprise a few of my orchestra colleagues played some of our favourite music. I looked at Will and in his eyes I saw the promise of the life I had always wanted. The lonely sadness of the orphanage was completely behind me.

We went on our honeymoon to the west of Scotland, Will's favourite place. We rode our bicycles along the coast and visited remote islands. The magic of the scenery enchanted me and we day-dreamed about building a house on one of the islands and even moving to Scotland when we had children. My most vivid memory was looking down from a cliff at the foam embroidery on the beach. He took me in his arms silently, but I could feel his heart crying with happiness.

When we returned to London, we rented a tiny flat close to the Academy. During the day we went our separate ways, but whenever we could, we would spend our evenings at home talking, listening to music and making plans for the future. My life was perfect.

Chapter 21

Ternate (Malay Archipelago), 19th century

Alfred Wallace had been travelling for several years around the western Pacific, visiting islands and countries that were quite different from his native England —and also from South America, where he had spent four exciting years. His job was to collect exotic species that he sold to European collectors. As a keen naturalist, he was doubly delighted to discover that his passion paid so handsomely.

In search of new treasures for his clients, in 1858 Wallace went to the Malay Archipelago, an area that reportedly contained 25,000 islands. It was between the Indian and Pacific Oceans, and largely unexplored by European naturalists. Eventually he reached a dense cluster of small islands of volcanic origin. After considering various options, he decided to stay in Ternate, at the northern end of the Archipelago.

The capital, also called Ternate, lay on a sandy coast at the foot of an active volcano. The most recent eruption had been 20 years earlier, and the town still hadn't fully recovered from it. Houses were single-storey with white stucco walls made of sago palm leaves, their roofs supported by strong wooden beams. The largest building was the Sultan's palace. He was the ruler of Ternate, and also of Tidore and Gilolo, two nearby islands that Wallace thought particularly promising for his collection.

Wallace found out about Ternate from reading the memoirs of Sir Francis Drake. He had been there in 1579, and described how the Sultan had met him under a canopy, accompanied by twelve lancers who said nothing but looked very fierce. He wore a crown of gold, and the fabric of his tunic was also threaded with gold. He had rings on all his fingers: rubies, emeralds and turquoises in his right hand, diamonds on his left.

The source of the Sultan's wealth was spices, and particularly cloves. For centuries, Ternate cloves were considered the best in the world, and Europeans longed for more of them. The largest plantations were on the main island, which was blessed with a deep-water port —ideal for the merchant ships that took the Spice Route to and from Europe. In time, though, other islands learned how to improve their cloves and other spices and the splendour of the Sultans started to fade. When Alfred arrived in Ternate, it was still an important port, but its glory days had passed.

Wallace had rented a house that he quickly made habitable, even comfortable. It had four rooms, two of which he filled with his specimens and taxidermy tools. On the patio there was fresh water —a cold well, a luxury in that climate— and fruit trees. A few minutes away there was a market where he could find milk, eggs, fish and a great variety of vegetables. When he wanted to take a break from his work, he walked around the island. With the beauty of its landscape, he was happy.

He had been living for several months in Ternate and was busy preparing some specimens to send to London when his servant announced a visitor:

—Mr Duivenboden is here.

—Let him in.

Wallace washed away the feathers and meat from the bird he was stuffing and went out to meet his guest.

Alfred knew a little about Mr Duivenboden. He was originally from Holland, had been educated in England and over the years had come to own half the crops in the island, a fleet of fishing boats and more than 100 slaves. Because of his vast wealth, he was nicknamed "The King of Ternate". Mr Duivenboden had exquisite manners and he loved literature and science; he seemed to have good relationships with everyone in the island, from the Sultan through to the humblest labourer. What brought him here today, Wallace wondered, as he greeted him.

—Good morning, Wallace —Mr Duivenboden bowed his head briefly—. I hope I am not disturbing you.

—Of course not. What can I do for you?

—Tonight I am giving a dinner at my house and I would like you to come. My sons are here and are keen to meet you.

—It will be a pleasure. Thank you for the invitation, I will be there.

Wallace arrived punctually at Mr Duivenboden's mansion. Following local tradition, the building was made of stucco with leaves and timber from the sago palm, but the architecture was incongruously Georgian, reminding Wallace of an English country house. The windows were open, and a fresh breeze ran through the house. Everything from the curtains to the furniture came from Europe, yet somehow managed to fit into this tropical setting.

—The Pacific hasn't changed your good English habits —said Mrs Duivenboden, glancing at her watch. She was slim and fair-skinned, with languid blue eyes, and she seemed quite at ease in these unusual surroundings.

—Thank you for inviting me —replied Alfred, following her into the drawing room.

Wallace felt comfortable with the Duivenbodens. Like him, they didn't come from the European aristocracy. Their success was due to their intelligence and long hours of hard work. Wallace knew only too well that many of the dinner invitations he received in England were motivated largely by an aristocratic affectation for an exotic guest.

—My dear Wallace —said Mr Duivenboden, coming into the room with his two sons—. Thank you for coming.

—It is a real pleasure.

—I would like to introduce you to Henry and Rupert. They have just arrived from England and are keen to meet you.

—Again, it's my pleasure —Wallace smiled at the two lanky young men—. Are you naturalists?

—No, Mr Wallace —replied Rupert, the eldest— my brother is a historian and I am a lawyer.

—Rupert is going to work with me —said Mr Duivenboden— and one day he will be in charge of the family business.

—You are famous in England, Mr Wallace —said Henry, his eyes sparkling—. Your work is highly respected; it is quite extraordinary how many new species you've found.

—You are flattering me. I'm not sure everybody would agree with you —replied Wallace.

Henry's comment reminded Alfred of the unpleasant discussions he had with his colleagues about his unorthodox belief in spiritualism. Because of that, the scientific establishment considered Wallace an eccentric naturalist who didn't deserve too much credit. His reputation had suffered because of his defiance of the status quo and his controversial opinions.

Alfred was fascinated by the paranormal. He believed in the power of hypnosis, crystal-ball reading, clairvoyance and the existence of ghosts. In common with many well-educated people from the Victorian age, Wallace was disappointed by the teaching of the Church of England. But neither did he accept the materialist view of the creation that some 19th-century scientists favoured: Wallace wanted to find a scientific explanation for all phenomena, both material and spiritual. His was a scientific quest, which included studying spiritualism from a logical and experimental point of view. In certain circles, though, these ideas had clouded his reputation as a scientist.

The arrival of the other guests brought Wallace back from his musings. Soon everybody was sitting down at the table, Alfred between the two sons, who swamped him with questions.

—Have you been to Gilolo Island? —asked Rupert.— It is one of the most interesting, but not well-known; we have been there several times, and it has completely different fauna from Ternate.

—Let Mr Wallace eat! —Mrs Duivenboden implored them.

—If you want to go, Mr Wallace —offered Duivenboden, undaunted—, you can use one of my boats. The captain is a young Chinese and has a crew of 12 slaves.

—What a handsome offer!—said Wallace, visibly excited by the idea—. When can we go?

—In a couple of days, which will give me time to prepare the boat.

Delighted with this plan, Wallace and the Duivenboden sons spent the rest of the evening discussing the expedition.

When the day came, they were supposed to leave at three in the morning, but the slaves didn't show up until five. When they all eventually arrived, the captain complained about their lack of punctuality, but it sounded as though he was joking about it; soon they were all laughing and talking as if nothing had happened. Wallace wasn't surprised; he now knew about the relaxed rhythm of life in the Malay islands, though it still bothered him.

When they arrived in Gilolo, again the indiscipline of the crew threatened to spoil the expedition. One of the strongest slaves refused to go inland with them. The captain had to beg him, and it took promises of lots of food and drink —and less work— to convince him. Trying to control his impatience, Wallace had started to unpack and find a place for the base camp. He chose the nearest hut, which was in a sorry state; but they would be staying for only five days, so he could put up with the filth and the bugs.

Every day Alfred headed into the jungle with Rupert and Henry; as the boys had promised, he was stunned by the diversity of species. The young Duivenbodens were good hunters and between the three of them they collected more than 100 species of insects, birds, reptiles and small mammals. They went out early in the morning to hunt, and in the afternoon organised and classified the specimens. Their activity fascinated the islanders, including an elderly imam, who followed them everywhere and even offered to help.

By the end of the trip, Wallace had collected more than 80 species of beetles, of which 43 were new to science. His biggest prize, though, was an unknown variety of the Paradise Bird. It had a metallic violet crest and an olive-green back with four white feathers attached to small bumps. With an emerald-green chest and yellow legs, it was the most beautiful bird Wallace had ever seen.

The expedition was more successful than Alfred could have hoped for. On the last day he decided to go at dawn to a part of the forest where he thought he had spotted a cat-like creature he hadn't seen before. After a long walk, mostly uphill, he heard the sound of running water and eventually came across a large waterfall tumbling down into a small pool.

He was puzzling over why he hadn't found the place before, when he turned and saw a man sitting on a rock by the lake. He had never felt threatened throughout his time in the Malay Archipelago, but instinctively he put his hand on his pistol and walked slowly towards him. The man sat there smiling, and then spoke:

—Don't be alarmed, Mr Wallace. I am exploring the area as well. I sat down to rest for a while —his voice was friendly.

—I didn't expect to see anybody in this part of the island —replied Alfred, surprised that the stranger knew his name.

The man was dressed for an expedition, but showed no signs of sweat or dirt on his clothes and his boots were polished. His English was impeccable, but his accent and features were not British. Wallace noticed his eyes, dark and bright like onyx.

—Do you mind if I walk with you? I would hate to miss the chance to spend time with the famous Alfred Russell Wallace.

—How do you know me?

—I have read all your articles. Your book on the Amazonian monkeys was fascinating. Besides, Mr Duivenboden is full of praise for you; he told me you would be in Gilolo.

—Do you know him?

—Yes, this is not the first time I have been to the archipelago. Don't you think it's extraordinary to find around here a man as interested in science as Mr Duivenboden?

—Yes, but he didn't mention anything about you — replied Alfred—. By the way, you haven't told me your name.

—Alexander Von Rossen. It is a pleasure to meet you. I have been following your career for a long time, so, if you don't mind, it would be a real honour for me to spend time with you in the forest.

—I don't see why not.

The two men started up the steep slope of the island's volcano, talking about the species they had seen on their trips.

—Are you a collector? —asked Wallace.

—No, I am not. My family has clove plantations in Tidore, so I come regularly to take care of the business. But my real interest in these islands is scientific. On that subject, one of your theories particularly intrigues me; you wrote that each species shows up in the same place as similar and pre-existing species.

176

Wallace was flattered. He hadn't realised his theories were known beyond a small group of friends and professors in England. He explained in detail how he had come to that conclusion.

—Tell me, Wallace, how many samples of a particular species do you collect?—asked Alexander.

—My clients want as much variety as possible, especially if something is exotic and beautiful. Other naturalists send one or two individuals; I often send as many as twelve. It is the best way to understand the characteristics of the same species.

—Don't you think it's peculiar?

—What do you mean?

—The variety within a species. Why aren't all individuals the same?

—I have asked myself the same question for years — replied Wallace, pleased that his companion seemed to understand so much—. The truth is that I ask myself several questions. Why and how species change over time, how do they adapt, how do they survive? Even more, why did some become extinct, as the fossil records show?

—I think you are asking the right questions —replied Alexander—. Have you ever read Malthus?

Alfred was surprised. He had read Thomas Malthus, but what had he to do with what they were talking about?

At that point, they heard a voice calling for Wallace.

—They must be looking for me, it's time for me to go.

—It has been a real pleasure to meet you, Mr Wallace.

—For me too. I would like to continue our conversation whenever you come back to Ternate.

—I would be delighted —replied Von Rossen, and, after shaking Alfred's hand, he disappeared into the jungle.

Wallace was deep in thought throughout the journey back to Ternate. As soon as they reached the island, he would ask Mr Duivenboden about Von Rossen. He had felt at ease with him, almost as much as he did with Bates, his companion during several expeditions down the Amazon.

While the boat was navigating through the dangerous channel between Gilolo and Ternate, Wallace kept thinking about Malthus. In his book An Essay on the Principle of Population, the famous 18th-century economist and demographer had argued that the size of a human population would always be limited by what he considered natural phenomena —wars, disease and famines. Could plants and animals be governed by similar constraints? Might that also explain why individuals of the same species varied?

When they eventually docked in the harbour at Ternate, Wallace bid farewell to his companions and went back to his house with his precious load. He felt exhausted and was starting to shiver; it seemed like, once again, he was going to get the fever. Even though the temperature was well above 30 degrees, Wallace felt cold.

He made some tea and went to bed under a thick blanket. Strange thoughts circled erratically in his feverish head, and images of Gilolo, birds, insects, butterflies, danced in front of his eyes. In one of his lucid moments, he remembered his conversation with Alexander: Malthus, population controls... maybe not all the newborns could survive ...what was that giant beetle doing in the bedroom? And perhaps that explained why there were variations within the same species ... The Paradise Bird revived and flew out of the window! ... And those variations separated permanently from their original relatives because only the best adapted survived.

As if in a flash, he was fitting together all his observations and speculations from his long years of study. The divergent lines separated from a primary species, but they were selected by natural controls and therefore changed over time; that was the reason why there were different fossils. Species were not fixed forms created by God, as the prevailing view suggested; they changed and kept changing and gradually became new species. Animal mimicry, allied species, instincts, feeding habits, sexual behaviour —all could be explained with this new theory. Despite his fever, Wallace could now grasp the ideas quite clearly.

He jumped out of bed; he had to write everything down before he forgot it. He spent two days and two nights at his desk; the high fever, instead of exhausting him, seemed to give him the energy to continue. At the end he had condensed all his thoughts into nine pages. He put them in an envelope and called for his servant to send it with the first boat to England. It would take months to get there, but the recipient, Charles Darwin, would understand what he was talking about.

When Darwin received Wallace's letter, he realised they had both reached the same conclusions on natural selection and evolution. Darwin and Wallace co-wrote a paper which was presented by Charles Lyell and Joseph Hooker at the Linnean Society in July 1858. Nowadays it is widely regarded as the most significant paper in the history of biology.

A year later, in November 1859, Darwin published the book he had been writing for 30 years: On the Origin of Species. It was Wallace's letter to Darwin that prompted the beginning of a revolution that changed forever man's place in nature.

Chapter 22

London, 21st Century

My life with Will was a joy. We loved each other, we understood each other and we had fun together. We both enjoyed travelling on the Continent, and I look back on a whirl of extraordinary trips together. In many ways, I still thought of myself as a girl from an orphanage in Malta, yet there I was in Prague, Paris, Rome, Munich and many more wonderful cities.

My reputation as a pianist was growing and even though the Academy continued to be my main base, I started to play with other orchestras too. One day Carol came into the studio where we were recording. She had a letter in her hand and her eyes were sparkling.

—I have wonderful news for you, Ariane.

Her tone of voice surprised me. She was usually calm, but that day she was unable to hide her excitement.

—You have been chosen as Young Performer of the Year by the magazine Classics!

I knew Classics very well. It was a monthly magazine, the bible for musicians in Britain, and I couldn't take in what she was saying.

—That means you have won a promotional tour in Europe and £10,000 in cash!

My colleagues crowded round, congratulating me as I took the letter from Carol.

"Dear Ms Claret:

It is a pleasure for us to write to you to let you know you have won the Amadeus Prize awarded every year by our magazine to a highly promising young artist. Congratulations!

Previous winners include Clara Tasquil and Martha Argerich, so you are in distinguished company.

The prize includes:

- The Amadeus Medal and Diploma

- A promotional tour in France, Germany, Italy and Austria, with all expenses paid

- A cash prize of £10,000

The chairman of Classics, Sir Les Thomas, will be in touch with you shortly to invite you to our offices.

With my best wishes and I do look forward to meeting you.

Olivia Hilton

Public Affairs Director

Classics Magazine"

I looked up at Carol and she hugged me tightly.

—You have a great future, Ariane —she whispered in my ear.

I immediately called Will and he hurried round to the Academy to celebrate with me.

—You are wonderful, Ariane, I am so proud of you. I always told you, you play like an angel and I'm not the only one who thinks that.

That night we went to our favourite Italian restaurant and laughed and hugged the whole evening. The waiters immediately sensed our mood, or perhaps Will had tipped them off about my prize. They brought a bunch of roses to my table, and one of them delighted the whole restaurant with an Italian aria. He had a beautiful voice and everybody clapped vigorously at his improvisation. Will and I sang all the way back home.

In the weeks after the prize was announced, I started to receive invitations from newspapers, TV and radio programmes. They all wanted to talk to me, a little girl from an orphanage in Malta. I took that sense of excited disbelief on my summer tour through Europe, and Will came with me. Neither of us could ever have guessed that, just a few months later, we would receive terrible news.

Chapter 23

Paris, 19th century

—What did you eat today? —Casimir's tone was serious. Marie said she didn't remember: —Something here and there.

He insisted:

—What did you eat?

The young woman looked at him, pale and fearless, but eventually she confessed: cherries and radishes. Casimir was furious with her, and with himself for allowing his sister-in-law to get into such a state. She had fainted in the middle of a physics lesson, but only that day she had told him she had fainted several times in her dingy flat in Rue Flatters. Casimir looked around. Marie's place had one small table that had to double as a writing and dining table, as well as a place where she kept her books, letters from her family, and some manuscripts. The bed was too small even for Marie's tiny frame. The chimney never warmed up and the roof was leaking. How could she live in these conditions? No wonder she got ill.

Marie had decided to live on her own, distancing herself from the loving but sometimes suffocating care of her sister Bronya and husband Casimir. Partly because she was always short of money and partly because she forgot, she ate very little and her health had suffered. Desperately pale, with dark rings around her eyes, she was showing all the signs of advanced anaemia: but what really worried Casimir was her dry cough. It could be yet another bout of tuberculosis.

Marie looked at Casimir without saying a word, her grey eyes defiant and an obstinate expression on her face. The young doctor sighed. He had no doubt Marie would continue to neglect her health. He had to do something drastic.

Maria Skłodowska was born in Warsaw in 1867 to a family of Polish intellectuals. Her father was a Physics professor and her mother the head of a prestigious girls' school. Both were passionate patriots and instilled in their four children a love for their country. At that time, Poland was run by the Russian Tsar, and for the Skłodowski family there was nothing more humiliating than having to accept his detested regime. Along with other intellectuals, they set up an underground resistance movement dedicated to preserving Poland's national identity. The Tsar's regime banned the teaching of Polish in schools, and all the text books were re-written to eliminate any reference to the past; but the Skłodowskis did everything they could to keep that pride alive.

It wasn't only patriotism that animated their family life. The parents, warm and loving, encouraged their children to revere knowledge. Dinner was a forum for scientific discussions, and the children grew up knowing that science was a force for progress and a way to liberate people from oppression.

Schools were also part of the national struggle. In the one that Marie and her sisters attended, teachers gave their lessons in Polish and taught the history and literature of their country. Whenever a Russian inspector showed up, the school caretaker alerted all the teachers with an agreed signal. The girls knew what they had to do: they quickly replaced their Polish text-books with knitting baskets, and switched the maps on the walls to the official ones. By the time the inspector came into the classroom, the girls were knitting and the teacher was reading a Krylov fairy tale in Russian.

Those visits were a double ordeal for Marie. Not only did she have to endure the presence of a hated symbol of the Russian oppression; as she was the cleverest girl in the class, the teacher always chose her to speak in front of the arrogant inspector.

—First the Prayer —he used to say, obviously bored. He couldn't care less about a bunch of annoying Polish girls.

Marie, in impeccable Russian, recited the Lord's Prayer.

—Name the members of the imperial family.

Marie, hiding her fury, listed their names.

—Who is our Emperor?

Pale and hesitating for a second, she replied:

—His Majesty Alexander II, Tsar of Russia.

Satisfied with this show of loyalty and the humiliation he knew he was imposing on them, the inspector left the room; he had other classes to torment. Each time this happened, the teacher took Marie in her arms to comfort her, while most of the other girls started crying.

When Marie finished school, she was not allowed to go to the men-only Warsaw University. Along with Bronya, her eldest sister, she registered at the "Flying University", a clandestine institute of higher education that accepted women students. After a while, frustrated by the difficulties of studying in secret, they both set their hearts on going to the Sorbonne in Paris. But how would they live there? Their father had lost all his savings in a speculative venture with his brother, and the meagre salary he received was barely enough to keep the family in Warsaw. Marie took a decision: Bronya would go to Paris to study Medicine, and she would stay behind in Poland working as a governess to support Bronya. With her knowledge of Polish, Russian, German and French, it wouldn't be difficult to find a job.

The years that Marie spent teaching at private homes left a wound in her soul. Not merely did her mother die, but she met people from her own country who were as mean as the Russian oppressor. After three years, saving all she could for Bronya, Marie had given up hope of getting to Paris herself. But her father never gave up. He wouldn't allow his daughter to waste her extraordinary brain, and he and Bronya persuaded Marie to travel to Paris and register at the Sorbonne. Bronya had already graduated and had recently married, and she and her husband would take care of her.

Initially, Marie had protested. She didn't want to leave Poland and abandon her father. But she consoled herself with the thought that she would eventually come back and look after him, and she kept that in the front of her mind as she boarded the third–class compartment on the train to Paris.

As the train trundled through the French countryside, Marie shook off the tiredness that came from sitting for three days in the foldable chair she had brought with her. She started to feel the exhilaration of freedom. Marie was met at the station by Bronya, newly pregnant with her first child, and her husband Casimir, and they took her to their home in the outskirts of Paris. Marie spent the first few months in a whirl of excitement; all her dreams were coming true. Although Bronya's home was small, she knew how to create a cosy atmosphere, and Casimir was always charming and enthusiastic. They often held musical events and political meetings with other Polish exiles. Surrounded by young people who, like her, were passionate about life, Marie was in her element.

On Marie's first visit to the Sorbonne, the white letters on the front door seemed like a charm to get her into a magic place:

École des Sciences, La Sorbonne

She had barely enough money for her first year's fees, and only one dress to wear, but Marie felt she was the luckiest person on Earth. She was the only woman studying physics, and her male colleagues were intrigued by this new arrival with the impossible surname. She arrived in the lecture room before everyone else and always sat in the front row. If anybody wanted to talk to her, she politely declined. Nobody could imagine that, behind that sad and serious face, with her thin and ashy hair, there was an extraordinary determination and an absolute conviction that science was the noblest calling.

Marie's routine was punishing. Even after many hours at work, Bronya and Casimir had to force her out of her room to get some fresh air. They wanted her to join in the gatherings they had at home, but Marie soon decided she hadn't come all the way from Poland for that. Before long, and partly to save the cost of travelling every day from her sister's home to the Sorbonne, she moved to a small room in the attic of a house in the Latin Quarter. There, Marie devoted herself to her studies. And there, inevitably, she got ill.

Bronya and Casimir realised the mistake they had made in letting Marie move out. This time, though, after she had a blackout during a lecture, they insisted she return to their flat at Rue d'Allemagne. Proper food, more sleep and some loving care were the cure that Marie needed, and even her dry cough disappeared.

Marie finished her year top of the class and, with the help of her family, she could continue her studies. She became the first woman in the history of the Sorbonne to graduate in physics. Although she knew it was time to go back to her homeland and her beloved father, the spell that knowledge had cast on her overcame her sense of duty. She wanted to stay another year at the Sorbonne to complete a course in Mathematics. When she discussed the idea with the family, they supported her. After all, she was postponing her return by only one year.

Her financial problems, though, hadn't disappeared. To teach at the Sorbonne was impossible for a woman, even though she was more competent than her male colleagues. One day, unexpectedly, she was asked to give Physics lessons in a girls' school in Paris. At last she had enough money to live on, and it wasn't long before her life changed again.

It was at the home of one of her professors that Marie met Pierre Curie. The young man's shabby elegance, his manners and even his scientific reputation didn't impress her. She was interested only in finding a new laboratory to work on some experiments that a group of Polish industrialists had asked her to perform. Pierre, by contrast, was immediately attracted to Marie. He was in his thirties, and hadn't yet found a woman who interested him. None had Marie's unusual mix: a passion for science, an extraordinary mind, an absolute determination and a graceful appearance.

It took him a long time to persuade her to marry him. Marie studied with the devotion of an ascetic; love, she had decided, was not for her. But Pierre was persistent, and she really felt easy with him; at times she even conceded that his soul was similar to hers. Eventually she accepted, and they married at the end of July. For their honeymoon they took a long cycling trip through the French countryside.

Now Marie was torn between her duty to her father and country, and her respect for Pierre's needs. He was prepared to follow her wherever she wanted to go, but she couldn't ask him to make that sacrifice. In France he was a renowned scientist, with his own laboratory and a brilliant career ahead of him. In Poland he would have to start from scratch, not least learning both Polish and Russian. Marie accepted that it was better to stay in Paris, at least for the time being.

Marie's decision was also influenced by her desire to complete a doctorate. A French physicist called Henri Becquerel had recently discovered a rock with traces of uranium. It produced rays that could go through anything except lead, and leave an impression on a photographic plate. Becquerel called the phenomenon X rays. Marie was fascinated by this discovery. She wanted to explore its origins, but to do that she needed a proper laboratory.

—We can ask Professor Lippmann, he might offer you a bigger space —suggested Pierre.

—Do you really think so?

Professor Lippmann had already let her use part of his laboratory for the tests she was doing for the Polish industrialists, but she doubted he would give away more of his precious space for a doctoral study.

In the event, Professor Lippmann didn't have much to offer. His own lab was too small for him, he said, but there was an old shed in the back that he could lend her. When Pierre and Marie saw it, their hearts sunk. It was a cluttered warehouse, with a dirt floor and a leaking roof. How could they work with X rays in that sort of place?

That was not enough to stop Marie. Her initial disappointment soon turned into determination, and a few weeks later both husband and wife were working full time on the project. They cleared out the shed and when they moved in they made sure the most sensitive equipment was well away from the holes in the roof. They didn't have enough money to fix everything or to buy a stove to heat the room. No matter: they were ready to study the mysterious rays.

When winter came and conditions in the shed became almost unbearable, Pierre, who had put aside his own research to concentrate on Marie's, was about to give up. She, though, was determined to continue.

While Pierre stayed at home to recover from a violent cough, Marie kept going to the laboratory. She was worried about her husband, but nothing would stop her going ahead with her experiments. One morning, a visitor came to the lab looking for Pierre.

—Madame Curie, I hope I am not bothering you —said the visitor—. I am passing through Paris and I hope to have the chance to meet Doctor Curie.

—He is not here. Is there anything I can help you with? —Her response was polite but distant. She didn't like to be interrupted while she was at work.

—We are doing some experiments with piezoelectric materials, and we know your husband is an expert in that field.

—It is better if you talk to him, but he will not be back here for a few days —she said.

—Oh, what a shame! —the stranger said—. If it is not an inconvenience, I would like to leave the results of our experiments.

—Leave them here and I will make sure he sees them —she said, distracted.

Marie glanced at the papers and was immediately struck by the patterns of piezoelectricity. Her eyes lit up, and some colour came back to her cheeks.

—Which elements is this material made of? —she asked, intrigued.

—We don't know. This is why we would like to ask Doctor Curie. It is very reactive, much more than quartz.

—Undoubtedly Pierre will be interested.

—That's what I thought.

They exchanged a few more remarks and the stranger agreed he would come back later in the week.

As he was leaving, he said:

—If you allow me, Madame Curie, you are the most admirable scientist in the world. Mankind is waiting for you.

Surprised by his remark and not a little flattered, Marie said goodbye. She saw him leaving the lab. With his aristocratic looks and perfect manners, the visitor didn't look like a typical researcher, she thought. Then she went back to her work and didn't think about him again.

When Alexander was asked how had it gone with Madame Curie, he answered with a smile:

—Fine, actually. She doesn't need us. She is on the right track and nothing will distract her. She is quite remarkable.

Marie Curie became the first woman to win a Nobel Prize, in physics. Later, she won another Nobel, this time for chemistry. She remains the only person to have won twice in different sciences. Her remarkable life was not limited to science. During the First World War, she developed X-ray mobile units to support field hospitals; she herself drove the units around the battlefields of France. But years of exposure to the lethal rays took a toll on Marie's health and she died of leukaemia at 66.

"Of all celebrated beings, Marie Curie is the one whom fame has not corrupted"

Albert Einstein

Chapter 24

London, 21st century

The first time Will noticed the lump in his neck, he was in his office. He had leaned down to pick up a piece of paper and felt a sudden pain. He touched his neck and felt a small, hard ball. At first, he didn't pay any attention to it. He was always healthy and athletic, and he was only 32. But the lump grew, to the point that he was having difficulty buttoning up his shirt and eventually I forced him to go to the doctor.

The day he got the biopsy results, he showed up at the Academy. I was in a rehearsal, and I was happy and surprised to see him behind the window talking to Anita. When I finished, I went out and both looked at me. She was in tears.

—What happened? —I asked, alarmed— Problems with your family, Anita?

—No, Ariane —Will sounded quite calm— it is not about Anita's family. It is me, I have cancer.

I dropped the music books I had in my hands and my head started spinning. By the time the doctors saw Will, the disease was very advanced and they told him he didn't have more than a year to live. Will wanted to enjoy the time left to him —to us— and so we arranged three magical days in Venice. We also spent two weeks in Scotland, visiting the places we had been to on our honeymoon.

To see him disintegrating in front of my eyes, becoming a bag of pain, was almost unbearable. Whenever I couldn't stand it any longer, I went to Elspeth's house to cry on her lap. She didn't say a word, she didn't ask any questions, she just stroked my head. Anita was also a great support, both for me and Will. She came every afternoon to visit; sometimes she stayed with him so that I could do other things; often, when he had chemotherapy sessions, she came with us to the hospital. Anita understood the agony of waiting for him to come out of the treatment room and she held my hands tightly.

Will's beautiful blond and curly hair became thinner and then he lost it completely; his bright blue eyes lay tired in his skull. But he never really lost his spirit and his only concern was for me.

—Don't stay on your own, Ariane —he said over and over again—,you are too young.

I could never reply. It was a titanic effort not to burst into tears.

—I only regret I didn't have a child with you —he said one day, looking out of the window from his hospital bed.

—When you get better … —I replied insincerely.

He tried to smile.

—Come here, Ariane.

I lay down by his side, we hugged each other and a short while later he stopped breathing.

The absurdity of his death was too cruel. He was supposed to live; we were supposed to have a home, a family; we were going to spend many years together. But I had come to think of him as just an interlude in my life, a life destined for desolation. Try as I might to keep going, I was overcome by bitterness and self-pity. Not even the piano consoled me.

I asked for leave from the Academy and spent the next two weeks wandering the streets of London, often until well past midnight. Back in the flat, I spent hours on the sofa staring at the ceiling. I didn't want to see anybody, not even Anita. Elspeth called me every day, and I couldn't bear to talk to her.

—How are you today?

—OK.

—I know it is very painful, but the worst thing you can do is isolate yourself. You are so young, you have so much to live for.

—Yes, thanks for the advice, goodbye—and I would put the phone down.

When I went back to the Academy, everybody was very kind to me, but I couldn't stand the sympathy from my colleagues and especially Anita's suffocating love. How could life continue when my world had been shattered?

197

Depression started to knit a thick and dark net around me, and the more time went by, the more pointless life came to seem. It was difficult to get up in the morning and even harder to go to work. I was fed up with rehearsals; I couldn't cope with the orchestra. As soon as I could, I hurried back to the flat, turned off the lights, shut the curtains and lay in bed for hours. I started to miss rehearsals, and eventually I stopped going to the Academy at all. Sleeping seemed the only reasonable thing to do, to sleep until I died.

Each time I woke up, I wanted a way to go back to sleep. I started with flu pills, then discovered that anti-histamines were more effective, especially mixed with vodka. One day there was a knock at my door. It was Carol and Mr Grace. Before I could stop them, they had pushed themselves inside.

—Ariane, we are very worried about you —said Carol, looking at me concerned—. The director told us that you are not going to the Academy. Please, let us help you.

—I am fine, thank you. I just had a cold, but it is almost gone now. I will go back on Monday —I noticed they were looking at the bottles and the empty pill bottles.

—Maybe you need to talk to somebody, a counsellor, a psychologist —said Carol.

—I don't think so. I don't need anybody —I replied, turning my back on them. But in doing so, I bumped into the table, tripped and fell over.

When I saw myself lying on the floor and the horrified look on the face of Mr Grace and Carol, I burst into tears. I had reached my limit, hit bottom and the options I had now were die or get out. I decided to get out.

Chapter 25

Siberia, 21st century

Zardoff stared out of the window at the frozen landscape, so familiar and so comforting. His fortress in the middle of the Siberian steppes had been a summer house of the imperial family before being expropriated by the Bolsheviks. Zardoff had played his part in the Revolution, helping the leaders of the uprising in Siberia. Years later, they had given the house to Zardoff, commenting that no one in their right mind would ever want to go there. It was exactly what Zardoff was looking for. From the day he had set eyes on the house, he had spent most of his time there, with only his servants and bodyguards as company. This was where he felt safe.

He didn't change a thing in the mansion. The French furniture, the silk carpets, the velvet curtains, the Meissen china, —even though the Tsar had rarely used the place, it was in its way a gem. Zardoff added a few exquisite paintings from his own collection, most of which he had stolen. For the rest, he loved things as they were.

There was no modern heating and most of the chimneys were never used. Zardoff preferred to be cold; his mind and body worked better that way. His paranoia —he had lots of enemies, he was sure of that— meant he could hardly bear to be with human beings. The solution was to keep as far away from so-called civilisation as possible, and this fortified house was exactly what he needed.

The mansion was not the only asset he owned. In fact, Zardoff was extremely rich, with properties all over the world. A stranger would simply have marked him down as an eccentric billionaire, but that was only a small part of what made Zardoff different.

***

He had been born in late 700 AD to a rich family in Moravia. From an early age, he had shown an extraordinary capacity to learn and understand complicated concepts. As he grew up, he also became a skilful fighter. He never got on with his father, so Zardoff was happy to leave home when Pyros chose him to be one of his students.

He would have been the ideal successor to Pyros, except for a fatal flaw: he despised every form of life, and particularly human beings. When he found out from Pyros about his special bloodline and his latent skills, Zardoff's contempt for ordinary humans grew. Although he could see that human beings had some level of consciousness, they were territorial, primitive and violent. It was a waste of time to try to help them, Zardoff had concluded. It was better to annihilate them or, at most, use them as slaves.

Zardoff's final break with Pyros came when the older man chose Alexander as his successor. Zardoff was furious. He and a few other dissidents created their own fraternity —the Superiors— whose objective was to destroy the Guides' work. Where the Guides inspired knowledge,

Zardoff disseminated intolerance and blindness; where the Guides advanced ideas of social progress, Zardoff promoted hatred and fanaticism.

It wasn't difficult for Zardoff to convince unscrupulous rulers that an alliance with him would be beneficial. He promised them wealth and power, and few could resist his arguments. He was also known to be ruthless with his enemies; nothing gave him more pleasure than to torture and kill.

His best allies were those religious and political leaders who manipulated their followers in the name of a homeland or a god when in reality they were just feeding their own hunger for wealth and power. Through them, and over many centuries, Zardoff had inspired wars, religious persecutions, intolerance and ethnic cleansings, all with the sole purpose of mankind's self-destruction.

For him, the greatest prize was to convert a Guide to his cause, and Sebastian had been his most important convert. It had not been easy to win him over from Pyros's side, but eventually he had turned him into a lackey. Sebastian had served him well for many years.

But now, with the end so close, he was failing —to the point that Zardoff had started to suspect that Sebastian was sabotaging his plans. He guessed Sebastian had regrets about leaving Pyros, but every time Zardoff had scrutinised his thoughts he perceived only a terrible fear. With that fear as his instrument, Zardoff could control Sebastian and get him to do exactly as he wished.

Chapter 26

London, 21st century

They weren't my real family, of course, but during those ghastly months, Elspeth and Anita showed me what it meant to have a mother and a sister. They took it in turns to make sure I was never alone, and Elspeth fiercely insisted that I ate properly. Carol was also a great support. She changed my engagements with the Academy, reducing the hours of practice and finding replacements for me on several tours. She often came to see how I was doing, and I knew she cared for my welfare in every way she could.

Once a week I went to see a therapist, a clear-eyed woman with a gift for asking simple questions. With her I unravelled, layer by layer, all the pain accumulated during my childhood and through the agony of losing Will. It was a heart-breaking process and I was thankful that she didn't allow me to wallow in my grief. Horrible things happened to people and it was nobody's fault. The sooner I accepted that reality, the easier it would be to move on. Through long hours of talking, I came to realise that, after all, I wasn't as helpless as I thought.

Gradually, my sadness —and my resentment of life— subsided. A year after Will died, I could face a new reality: even if I missed him every second of the day, I couldn't do anything to bring him back; I could only move on.

Throughout that year, I hadn't touched anything in the flat. The flowers he gave me were still in the vase, shrivelled and brown; the books we read together were lying on the coffee table; his clothes were hanging in the cupboard; even the spider webs that grew around his desk went unchallenged. Then, one spring morning, I started to clean up and decided to give away what I didn't need. Eventually, the only sign of Will was his photo in our bedroom. Although his shadow followed me everywhere, it was a comfort; it encouraged me to keep going.

I went back to life at the Academy, practicing and playing in concerts. To keep busy in my spare time, I started giving private lessons to children. My first student was Helena, Elspeth's granddaughter. At that time she was ten, much changed from the little girl I met when I arrived in London. I went to her house every Tuesday after the Academy, and sometimes I stayed for dinner. It was a chance to get to know Emily who, like her mother, felt she was entitled to protect me and feed me.

I became Helena's confidant. She was a precocious child, her head full of romantic dreams, and every month she was in love with someone new. Sometimes she had a crush on a schoolmate, but mostly she preferred to love from a distance. Her particular passion was the young English boybands. She knew all their songs and wanted to learn to play them on the piano. She showed me the newspaper cuttings of such and such a singer, on which she painted hearts, stars, flowers and even verses. I had to keep her on track so as not to waste time during the piano lesson. I couldn't help comparing how dull and arid my life had been at ten; it was fun to go back in time and live a borrowed childhood. Helena and I became real friends and, sometimes, when her parents went to their Cotswolds house for the weekend she stayed with me at my flat.

Helena never knew how much she helped me to recover.

***

When I heard there was an opening at the Vienna Music Academy, I asked Carol and Mr Grace for their advice. Both thought I should apply: this would be an excellent opportunity and not only for my career. After several auditions and interviews, I left London at the beginning of September. It was exactly six years since I had arrived in England. I would be taking Will in my heart; I no longer needed to be in his country to feel close to him.

I rented a flat with a small balcony and views onto the Prater. I met new people and I learned a lot from the orchestra conductor, Andrés Montero. He was a talented Venezuelan, and I soon became friends with him and his wife Susana. They often invited me to their house, and I had a lot of fun with their two children, both musical prodigies. I enjoyed the warmth of a Latin American home; it was helping me to get over Will's loss.

After two years, when my contract expired, Andrés offered me a permanent post, but I realised I was starting to miss England. Anita had been out to stay with me, always insisting the Academy wasn't the same since I left. She was tempted to go back to Naples, hoping to find a place in the San Carlo, the opera house. I also knew that Carol, Elspeth and Mr Grace were hoping I would return. I decided to return to London, and at the beginning of the summer I was back in my flat. The tenants I had had for two years, a young Swiss couple, left the house in immaculate condition. They had painted the walls in light colours and changed the curtains and the lampshades. They asked me if I wanted the flat restored to its original state, and I was relieved to hear myself immediately saying no. I wanted to keep their changes. I was ready to start a new life.

Chapter 27

Shanghai, 21st century

In her house in the French Quarter of Shanghai, Fiammetta picked up the envelope that had just arrived in the post. She knew immediately that it was from Alexander. His handwriting was from another century, precise and elaborate. She put the envelope on the lacquered cabinet. She didn't need to open it; she knew it would be an invitation to go to Roshven. It made her realise how much she had missed her friend, the man who had guided her so cleverly, who had believed in her when others thought she was a traitor. He was a legendary Guide of Time, the best of all.

She looked out of the window at the garden. Fine rain was falling on the pond, which was covered by water lilies and surrounded by rocks and bamboos. Her favourite place was the small pavilion in the middle of the pond, reached by a wooden bridge.

How many years had she lived in China? A few decades, anyway. When Mao died, she moved there to help recover what was left of the country's ancient history after the havoc of the Cultural Revolution. The old dictator and his followers had destroyed almost everything of beauty; they had imprisoned many artists, and intimidated most of the rest.

Even now, the government still controlled so much that it tried to stifle any art it didn't like. As Fiammetta had done so often before, she managed to help many artists, shielding them from the authorities, smuggling their work out of the country, giving them encouragement and often money as well.

That had been her mission throughout the centuries: to be the muse of painters and sculptors, sometimes as a model, often as their protector and patron. She had travelled widely, playing a significant part in the flourishing of the arts. Now her time in China was nearly over. After moving to Shanghai, Fiammetta had hired a young woman, Mei Yanping, to be her personal assistant. Or at least that was what she had told her. Mei had turned out to be what Fiammetta hoped for, and she would soon become her successor. The girl was talented and intelligent and, most important of all, she understood artists. Her father was a painter executed by the Maoists for his "counter-revolution bourgeois art"; her mother disappeared shortly afterwards. Little Mei was raised by her aunt, who had helped her to develop her talent.

Fiammetta knew a lot about the young woman. When she was looking for her successor, Mei was the one with the strongest bloodline. Fiammetta had met her at the Shanghai Art School. When she traced her bloodline, she realised that Mei had the potential to become a Guide, and maybe, one day, her successor.

A light knock at the door roused Fiammetta from her thoughts.

—Come in —she said.

Mei had a portfolio under her arm and she leaned forward to greet Fiammetta.

—I would like to show you what I have done at the school.

Mei studied Chinese traditional painting and she specialised in the Xieyi technique, one of the few traditions that had survived the cultural holocaust. Its purpose was to show the union between man and the Cosmos. In the Xieyi tradition, it was more important to represent feelings than images; Mei's paintings, with their subtle and delicate lines, expressed her profound reverence for Nature.

—This is wonderful! —said Fiammetta—.You should have an exhibition.

—Yes, I have discussed some ideas with my professor —replied Mei—, and some of my work will be in an exhibition in the Xi Yapong gallery. He has invited several art critics.

Fiammetta smiled. Her pupil wasn't only talented, she knew how to move in artistic circles. One day, she felt sure, Mei would become a famous painter.

—Today is the day —said Mei, changing the subject suddenly—, this time there's no excuse.

Fiammetta sighed.

—Yes, I know. We shouldn't keep postponing it. Besides, Mei, soon we'll need to talk about my trip.

—I suppose so —replied Mei, though she didn't want to accept it. She was devoted to Fiammetta, and the thought that she might be leaving tormented her. But she knew it was inevitable. Her Guide had to continue with her journey.

—Let's not talk about it —said Fiammetta. Then, changing her tone—: I know you are very curious to see the portraits.

—Yes! I want to see them all! —Mei was genuinely enthusiastic.

Fiammetta went to an old trunk in the corner of the room. It had golden figures painted on it, and a two-pointed feather on the lock. She opened it. It was full of art books.

Fiammetta took a book out of the trunk and said:

—This was the first one.

Mei glanced at the open page and then gasped in surprise. In the Botticelli painting from the 15th century, The Birth of Venus the woman's face was unmistakable: it was Fiammetta.

Chapter 28

Scotland, 21st century

The orchestra's tour of Scotland was unexpected. Every autumn for many years, Carol had organised a series of concerts in the south of England, but one of the most generous sponsors of the Academy had asked her to include some Scottish cities as well. Our plans were ambitious: in the space of just three weeks we were going to play in Aberdeen, Edinburgh, Glasgow, Stirling, Inverness, Perth and finally on Skye.

We started in Aberdeen on a grey Monday at the end of October. Anita was on the tour as well, and that filled me with mixed feelings. I always enjoyed her sense of fun, but I wasn't sure that she would be the best person to help me face the inevitable difficult memories.

Half way through the tour, we had a few days off to relax which I badly needed. Anita, though, had other ideas. She seemed more restless than usual and insisted that, instead of staying with the rest of the orchestra, we should head for a small village on the west coast, in the middle of nowhere. The view, she said, was the most beautiful in Scotland. We could take long walks during the day and go to the pub at night. Reluctantly, I agreed.

As dusk was falling, we reached a bed and breakfast in a village called Glen Lui. Across the grey sea, we could see Skye. The place had been a boat house and then been expanded into an ample and welcoming lodge. The owners welcomed us by a roaring fire, and I caught a whiff of malt whiskey. Our room was small but warm and comfortable. There were flowers on the table, and a small bathroom off in one corner.

The next morning I woke up early, and looked out of the window. The view was so much like my first day in Scotland with Will. From the lodge I could see dark clouds threatening. There was dew on the grass, and the trees were stark against the leaden sea.

For a long while I sat by the window, lost in nostalgia. When Anita woke up, we went downstairs for breakfast, drawn by the smell of fried eggs. We decided to visit the grave of a local heroine who had apparently fought against the English, been taken prisoner and then burnt alive. It sounded really gruesome, and I would have been happier to stay in and read a book. But Anita insisted, and Anita usually got her way.

We climbed a steep hill, to find only a small and neglected grave —but the view was breathtaking. In the distance, on the other side of the bay, we could see a large granite-grey house.

—That must be Roshven Castle. Do you think people live there? —I asked Anita.

—Well, our landlord told me that a Baron lives there. Generous but strange, apparently. Anyhow, let's keep moving, we can't stand here.

—I want to stay here for a while. Since when were you a fanatic about exercise? —I asked.

—I will explain later —she said, with a playful smile—. You will freeze if you don't move.

—Don't worry, I will stay just a few minutes. I'll see you back at the lodge.

—OK, I am going to walk to the lighthouse and back.

Anita left, and I sat on a stone and gazed out at the sea. The rocky coast, the waves crashing on the shore, the salty breeze, —they took me back to a time when I was happy. Will had taught me to love this barren and haunting landscape, where it was easy to believe that a prehistoric monster lived in the bottom of a lake or that three witches lived in a forest, as described in Shakespeare's MacBeth.

It was starting to rain and I decided to leave, walking towards Roshven Castle. I had read that it was one of the oldest buildings in Scotland, built around the year nine hundred as a fortress to protect the region from the Vikings. As I made my way down a slippery path towards it, I lost my balance and fell. I must have hit my head on a rock, and I do remember lying there for some time, in pain, wondering if I had cracked my skull. When I eventually opened my eyes, there was a man staring down at me.

###

Acknowledgments

Several people were kind enough to read early drafts of this book: Carolina Afán de Rivera, Dalgi de Berardinis, Hernán Castellanos, Johanna Hohle and Alfonso Riascos. I am also grateful to Ascanio Afán de Rivera, who tried very hard to make me understand particle physics; to Natalia Moreno who proof-read the book; to Ned Pennant-Rea who made me rethink some of my assumptions; and to my husband, Rupert Pennant-Rea. He is not only the best editor in the world; he is also the best husband in the world.

About the book

Thank you for your interest in The Guide of Time. If you enjoyed it, I' d be very grateful if you wrote a review for your favourite retailer. Thank you!

The seeds of The Guide of Time were sown many years ago when I was studying science at university. I came to realise that great discoveries were always a combination of hard work, serendipity and inspiration. Of the three, inspiration was the one that most intrigued me. Scientists often describe the solution to a problem they have been working on as the appearance of an idea out of nowhere, a ray of light that comes to them with dramatic suddenness and a sense of certainty. Where do these ideas come from? What if mankind has been guided by some unseen hands? The answer to these questions is the essence of the trilogy of The Guide or Time.

But who are the Guides of Time? The idea of a superior human race came from an exhibition in London about the discovery of 800,000-year-old footprints in Happisburgh, eastern England. They were the oldest human prints ever found outside Africa, and they belonged to a group of perhaps five humans, a mixture of adults and children, probably a family. The footprints were found heading south along the bank of what was the River Thames –which at that time ran through Norfolk and out to sea at

Happisburgh, before the Ice Age pushed the Thames further south. These people were hunter-gatherers and a different species to ourselves, although their exact identity is uncertain. They may well have been trying to escape from the Ice Age. What if, to shelter from the freezing cold, they found refuge in caves and developed an underground settlement?

This idea is supported by the vast European network of tunnels what weaves from Scotland to Turkey. Although these were created relatively recent compared to the Happisburgh dwellers, they pose an intriguing question about human life underground. German archaeologist Dr Heinrich Kusch, in his book "Secrets of the Underground Door to an Ancient World" (Original title in German: " Tore zur Unterwelt: Das Geheimnis der unterirdischen Gänge aus uralter Zeit ... ") explained that these tunnels were dug under hundreds of Neolithic settlements all over Europe and the fact that so many have survived 12,000 years indicates that the original networks must have quite extensive and well built.

Dr Kusch states in his book that in Bavaria in Germany alone they have found 700 metres of these underground tunnel networks and in Styria in Austria 350 metres. Across Europe there were thousands of them -from the north in Scotland down to the Mediterranean. The tunnels are quite small, measuring only 70cm in width, which is just enough for a person to crawl through. In some places there are small rooms, storage chambers and seating areas!

While many believe Stone Age humans were primitive, incredible discoveries such as the 8000 year-old temple

Gobekli Tepe in Turkey and, more recent, Stonehenge in England -which demonstrate advanced astronomical knowledge -indicate that they were not simple hunters-gatherers as initially thought.

The real purpose of the tunnels is still a matter of speculation. Some experts believe they were a way of protecting man from predators while others believe they were a way for people to travel safely, sheltered from harsh weather conditions or even wars and violence.

In a recent trip to Iran, I ventured, through a vertical shaft 30m underground, in a Qanat, a small tunnel part of a vast network across the Persian empire used to transport water from an aquifer. Qanats created a reliable supply of water for human settlements and agriculture in a dry and hot climate.

So, underground human activity used to be quite dynamic in the past. What if, to shelter from the freezing cold, a group of our ancestors found refuge in caves? And what if they managed to develop an entire civilisation underground, more advanced than our own?

These are the questions that started me thinking about this book. Writing it has taught me a lot, and I hope you will enjoy reading it.

About the Author

Cinzia De Santis was born in Italy and moved to Venezuela as a baby. She studied Biology, had an exciting career in business and now devotes her time to her passions: books and travelling. She had previously also been an actor, performing both as an amateur and a professional, and it was then that she started writing short stories in Spanish. Cinzia moved to England in 2003 and now lives in London . The Guide of Time is her second novel in English. More about Cinzia and her books at: www.cinziadesantis.com

Bibliography:

Chapter 9

Brahmagupta, 628. About the Right and Established Doctrine of Brahma, known in Hindu as Brahmasphutasiddhanta

O'Connor, John J.; Robertson, Edmund F., "Brahmagupta", MacTutor History of Mathematics archive, University of St Andrews

Chapter 11

Tess Anne Osbaldeston. 2000. Pedanius Dioscorides: De materia medica. Ibidis Press. Originally written in the 1st century of the common era.

Chapter 15

S. Frederick Starr, 2013. Lost Enlightenment. Princeton Press, pp 466.

Chapter 19:

Rossi, P. 2006. Il tempo dei maghi. Raffaello Cortina Ed. p. 5.

Roberts, R. 1989. Serendipity: Accidental Discoveries in Science. John Wiley & Sons Editions.

Barrett, D. 2007. Secret Societies. Constable and Robinson.

Chapter 21:

Wallace, A.R. 1858. The Malay Archipelago. MacMillan Press.

Wallace, A.R. 1847. Miracles and Modern Spiritualism. Kessinger Publishing.

Chapter 23

Curie, Eve. 1937. Madame Curie. A biography. Da Capo Press.

Other Sources

You can find out more about scientific inspiration in these links:

www.paperveins.org

www.dreaminterpretation-dictionary.com/albert-einstein

www.wikipedia-Newton occult studies.com

www.brainpickings.org

Connect with me:

My website: http://cinziadesantis.com

Twitter: @cinziadesantis_

Facebook:
https://www.facebook.com/cinziadesantis2016/

https://www.instagram.com/santiscinziade/

https://www.youtube.com/dashboard?o=U